Rattling to Ramsey

A collection of Isle of Man Short stories

by Judith C Davis

Published by **mallardsmanxbooks**
9 Athol Court, Port Erin, Isle of Man, IM9 6EJ.

Printed by Quine & Cubbon Ltd., Athol Street, Port St Mary, IM9 5DS.

ISBN 978 0 9576097 0 9

Front cover photograph courtesy of Mycl Corrin

CONTENTS

Earlier versions of Stories 1,4,5,8 and 11 were published in 'The People's Friend.' Story 3 was published in Woman's Weekly.

These stories are fictitious as are the characters within them, their opinions are sometimes mine, but usually theirs.

Introduction

This is a diverse selection of stories, some new, some previously published. As in 'Climbing to Cregneash,'(2004) the stories are locally set, their origins evolving from associations and experiences gleancd from life. The Isle of Man has always been my home and my love for Ellen Vannin as well as my fondness for 'character' is, I hope, apparent in my writing. When I was a child the Isle of Man was truly a holiday isle, with a short season. Summers were fun and lively; winters were quiet and for many, hard. Nowadays I appreciate the vibrant atmosphere of Manx life throughout the year, the vast improvements in health services, travel and living conditions. It is good to treasure the past, and often comforting to wallow in nostalgia, but would anyone sacrifice central heating and technology for a smoky chiolliagh fire? The precious elements of our island remain unchanged; the grandeur of our hill tops, our glens, hidden valleys and glorious beaches with their crashing tides. May your enjoyment of these stories encourage you to re-explore every location.

Judith Carol Davis

April 2013

A BUSINESS ARRANGEMENT

Sulby

My earliest memories are of the nineteen fifties. I recall sweets coming off ration and the simplicity of domestic life compared to today, primitive kitchens, wooden draining boards and coal fires. Few households had telephones, home made clothing and knitwear was the norm and my parents and teachers constantly alluded to 'the war.'

As a post war child I was unaware of the dislocation of those years though my sister remembers barely knowing 'Daddy' when he returned from active service. Adjusting to post war life must have been difficult, especially for families whose menfolk did not return.

My Great Uncle, Ernest Corlett of Ballaugh, fought in the First World War, his pencilled letters home reveal his longing for the Island; his memorial stands in Ballaugh churchyard. He never came back to farm the land he loved.

My father Sydney Shimmin Corlett served in North Africa, Italy and Norway and although he returned physically intact the memories of his experiences and lost comrades never faded. Such heroes knuckled down and coped with peace-time life. Likewise the war widows, their fine men gone, they had no choice but to get by.

Sometimes though, the need for a man became more than even a strong minded woman could bear.

1

Lizzie Crellin surveyed herself doubtfully in the mirror of the battered dresser. "Well, I've made as much of meself as can be done in the time, an' no man, not even Gregory Killen can ask more than that."

Lizzie's long, narrow, rather solemn face lit with a smile as her mind settled, as it so often did nowadays, on Gregory Killen. He was no Adonis, he was only a little man, but he was cheerful and kind and Lizzie had decided, definitely, that he would do.

"So, tonight we'll get things sorted," Lizzie said, getting up briskly and pulling a cardigan about her. The old farmhouse was draughty at the best of times and tonight, if she wasn't mistaken, there was going to be a hard frost.

"Just in time for Christmas," Lizzie said cheerfully as she clattered downstairs. She hurried into the kitchen, checked the fire was well banked up and looked around the cosy room with a pleased eye. Over the past few days she'd given the place a right good clean, for you never knew who'd call over the festive season. The cake and biscuit tins on the dresser were full. The holly along the picture rail was bright with red berries. The spruce tree on the sideboard was laden with baubles and home made gingerbread. Christmas was a time to be cheerful, even if luxuries were still on ration. Winter was long, and folk needed a holiday to lighten their spirits.

Nevertheless, as the clock struck and the sound echoed around the empty farmhouse Lizzie experienced a pang. Trimmings and festive touches were all very well, but nothing made up for loved ones gone.

"That dratted war," Lizzie sighed fretfully, nudging the fireguard closer to the coals before hurrying to fetch her best coat.

2

At the village hall Gregory would be waiting for her. It wouldn't do to be late. There was business to settle between them.

When, four months before, Gregory Killen had started paying her attention, Lizzie had wondered what he was after. Everyone knew that he'd been under his mother's thumb all his life. The only time he'd got free was when he joined up, and hadn't old Mrs Killen given him a going-over for that! Some in the village thought Gregory wouldn't return to the island when the war ended. But home he'd come, to plough the small tenanted fields and do his best on their sour curragh land. Last year when Mrs Killen was taken into the Mannin Infirmary Gregory gave up the farm, and found a job in Ramsey. The locals had been surprised. They'd been even more surprised by his sudden attachment to Lizzie Crellin.

"You don't want to encourage him, Lizzie," May Barker, Lizzie's best friend had said, more than once. "All he's looking for is a cheap housekeeper an' a cosy place to live."

"That's not the way of it at all," Lizzie snapped, her cheeks flushing hotly, when May reiterated this opinion two days ago in the Sulby shop. Lizzie banged down a shilling for the loaf she was holding before wagging its crusty bulk in May's face. "You look to your Tom before meddlin' in my business, May," she'd retorted, before turning on her heel and stamping out.

Joe Corlett, the shop man was gawping. "What's the daft wummin plannin', May?"

May felt guilty about Lizzie and prevaricated, "Are these your best spuds?" She'd asked brusquely, in a diversionary tactic. Joe's retail hackles shot up. "They're good enough for your Tom. He allus eats like a sow troughin'. He'd not notice if they was moots or thistles!"

"What manner of ways is that to speak to a customer?" May shrilled.

"The way I always speak to them that's on tick. Would you like to settle your account, Mrs Barker?"

"Humph!" May grimaced. "I'll take three pound of spuds, an' I'll settle with you Friday."

"See you do," Joe said agreeably, "an' let me know how Lizzie gets on."

3

If Lizzie had realised that the village was watching the progress of her friendship with Gregory she might have been concerned, but then again, she might not. Lizzie was used to standing on her own two tough soled feet. She'd had to be. Her man, her fine, loving Harold hadn't returned from the war. So although this frosty evening she was excited, as any woman would be, at the prospect of an evening out which might end in an understanding, she had the consolation of knowing that if nothing came of this business between her and Gregory, she still had her farm, her livestock, and her self respect.

Nonetheless, she very nearly skipped out into the darkened yard towards her bicycle, a trusty machine that leaned against the house wall, winter and summer. Lizzie owned a wagon, but that needed petrol, and besides it was hardly suited to an evening out. The pig and sheep scented wagon was a workaday method of transport. A midnight cycle ride under the stars with Gregory at her side might work the necessary magic if, by then, Gregory hadn't come up to spec.

Lizzie had barely lifted one of her best shoes to the pedal when she was brought up short.

"Lizzie, you got a minute?"

Robbie Cooil's shout made Lizzie tut. "What is it, Robbie? I can't be hangin' about."

"Clara's not well, Lizzie. You should look at her."

Lizzie's excitement abated. Clara was her prize sow. "Oh my gum, what's up with the cra'tur?" Without a thought for her best dress, shining patent shoes and good tweed coat, Lizzie hurried into the pig shed after Robbie.

Clara, a massive, good-natured animal, was slumped on her side, looking glum.

"She's been strainin' this past hour, but there's nothin' doin'."

"Aw, what's up then, oul' dear?" At the sound of Lizzie's voice Clara stirred, and as Lizzie stroked her bristly flank a flicker of relief appeared in Clara's tiny eyes.

4

"There, there," Lizzie soothed. "You're right, Robbie. She's needin' a hand, I reckon."

Robbie shuffled his Wellington boots on the straw covered concrete.

"I know, lad. You get off. I'll stay." Robbie had a wife who would give him jip if he didn't turn up in time to take her to the Christmas social.

"Jus' hang on a minute while I get my boots and overall, Rob, there's a boy." As Lizzie darted into the house, to throw off her good coat and shoes, her anxiety over Clara outweighed her disappointment. It was a shame sure enough, but these things happened. She just hoped that Elspeth Quine wouldn't attempt to collar Gregory while he was in a soft mood. Elspeth had been hunting a man for more years than anyone could remember. Up till now her targets had more sense than to let her catch them. "Just tell Gregory what's amiss, Robbie, would you?" She said as she re-emerged into the farmyard.

"I'll do that, Lizzie, right enough," Robbie nodded, leaping onto his rattletrap bike. For a moment Lizzie watched the beam of his cycle lamp waver along the lane, and then she turned towards the barn, shivering, for the air was icy. Before going inside she glanced up at the brilliant stars sparkling overhead. It was a real Christmas sky.

As Lizzie settled beside the old pig her thoughts slipped back to other Christmases; jolly, noisy occasions when she'd been little, quieter Christmases as her parents got older, then her best Christmas, just before the war, when she and Harold had spent their first Christmas together. And then the war came...

Lizzie didn't often let herself dream about what might have been. Harold had been her husband for no more than two years when she received the telegram telling her he'd been killed in action. Sometimes, looking back, it seemed but a dream marriage, as though the whole episode was something out of a storybook, a sixpenny romance, borrowed from the circulating library.

5

"But he was real, all right, an' a lovely man, Clara. If he'd come back I might have been the mother of a fine brood of sons and daughters myself, by now."

Clara groaned and strained again and Lizzie set her mind to the matter in hand. It was all very well reminiscing about times gone by, but dreaming didn't get pigs delivered, and she was not so well off that she could afford to lose a litter of porkers at any time of the year.

A remarkably short time later Lizzie was looking down with pleasure at nine wriggling piggy tails as they fought their way to Clara's milk. The piglet that had caused all the bother, a solid porker of more than usually wide girth, was already guzzling contentedly, and Clara, her work and duty done, was slumped peacefully, with closed eyes and what looked remarkably like a smile on her porcine face.

Lizzie felt pleased too and was washing her hands and arms in an icy bucket of water when she was startled by footsteps in the yard. She reached for a piece of sacking to dry herself.

"Lizzie, there you are."

Lizzie's heart thumped with surprise. Gregory Killen stood in the doorway, outlined against the starry sky. His shy smile, as he came nearer, made Lizzie's chest tighten, as though she was a callow girl again. "Well, it's nice to see you, Gregory. I thought you'd be dancin' the night away."

"No, I'd not be doin' that, Lizzie, not without you there."

Lizzie was surprised by the intensity in Gregory's voice. A moment before she'd been picturing Elspeth Quine manoeuvring him submissively towards the village hall mistletoe. Now he was beside her, and he seemed far from submissive.

"Robbie told me about the sow. I came to see could I help." Gregory cast a smile at the guzzling piglets. "But I see you managed fine."

"Yes," Lizzie said proudly. "I did." She knew she sounded self-satisfied, but that could not be helped. There was no shame in being pleased with what you did well. "But thank you for coming, Gregory. I know you were a good pig man in your time."

Gregory came closer; together they looked down on the new family. "I miss the livestock, Lizzie. I miss the farm, too, truth to tell."

Lizzie didn't respond to this. She could almost hear the rest of his admission in his voice. He didn't miss being constantly barracked by his old mother. The poor man, Lizzie thought, with sudden compassion. What sort of a life has he had up till now?

"We'll go inside," she said briskly. It would be no good if she let her emotions get the better of her. My goodness, she was too old to feel moony over any man. She had a business arrangement to get sorted. However, good manners prompted her to add: "I'm sorry you're missing the Christmas social, Gregory."

"That's no matter, Lizzie. No matter at all." Gregory surveyed Lizzie with his kindly brown eyes, and again Lizzie felt that strange feeling beneath her ribs as she led the way out of the barn. "You didn't have Elspeth Quine pestering you then?" She said, as she made a show of latching the door. "She's had her eye on you for years."

"Has she? No. Once I knew you weren't coming then I felt there wasn't much point in staying." Gregory's brown eyes flashed another tender look. Good gracious, Lizzie thought, as she pushed open the farmhouse door, the man's got confidence enough for ten tonight. Has he been drinking?

As Lizzie gestured Gregory to a chair and went to the scullery to give her hands a good scrub she wondered was she wise, entertaining him in such a mood. Perhaps she should send him home to cool off. She had thought to dictate to him, not the other way around.

"You'll take tea, Gregory," Lizzie said, when she came back into the kitchen, the filled kettle in her hand.

"I'll not say no, Lizzie, though there're things we need to discuss. Sit down, Lizzie, dear." Gregory reached and took the kettle from Lizzie and put it gently on the hob. "There, it'll boil when it's ready, and if you still want me to have a cup of tea when we've talked, that'll be grand."

Gregory smiled expansively, and seemed suddenly at ease, looking round the kitchen with an appreciative eye. "You've got a fine place here, Lizzie. An' you've got it done up right nice for Christmas."

"I have that." Lizzie said shortly, deciding to try to be polite rather than snapping his head off. Ordering her about in her own kitchen indeed, perhaps May Barker was right. Perhaps Gregory was just looking for a cosy place to live?

Lizzie didn't sit down, so neither did Gregory. "You're a grand, hard working woman, Lizzie Crellin, and I respect you for that."

Lizzie felt her throat tighten. How many years was it since Harold had said almost the same thing? Lizzie returned his look squarely. "That's nice of you to say, Gregory," she murmured, but then a rejoinder slipped out before she could help herself. "Is it respect for me or for the farm here, because much as I like you, Gregory, I think we deserve plain speaking?"

Gregory flushed and drew himself up to his full height. As he was a small man they were still not quite at eye level. "I think I love you, Lizzie Crellin," he said simply, "and if you'd do me the honour of becoming my wife I will do my very best to make you happy."

Lizzie flushed, but before she could answer, he went on. "I don't expect you to make over Ballavere to me, Lizzie, or anythin' like that. In fact, I've got another farm in mind that we could take on together, as equals, like."

"My, you've thought this out right enough," Lizzie gasped, embarrassed to realise how much she'd misjudged Gregory Killen. She had needed a man about the place, and Gregory had seemed to fit the bill. She'd pictured herself having to chivvy him into marriage. That Gregory might manage the situation, and have his own plans, she had not suspected. Yet, looking at him now, with his care worn face and his nice, but stubborn chin, she should have. He was no longer the shy boy she remembered from schooldays. He was a mature man who had seen six years active service in the war, and she'd heard he hadn't had an easy time.

"I won't be beholden to you, Lizzie. If we're to be married I want it to be on an equal footing. You'll not reject me, Lizzie dear, will you?"

8

Lizzie gripped the chair back in front of her. "Goodness, you're forthright tonight, Gregory Killen. You're quite taking my breath away."

"That was the idea," Gregory said, with a sheepish smile. "I've been working up to this for weeks, Lizzie, an' I had two stiff Sherries before coming out."

Lizzie chuckled. "I thought you were staunch temperance, Gregory."

"That sherry was enough to make me," Gregory confessed, "It was horrible stuff. It was a bottle the oul' woman had in for years."

"You could have poisoned yourself, Gregory," Lizzie exclaimed. "Sit down, lad," she smiled. "I'll fetch us a glass of my bramble wine. After all, it is almost Christmas."

As Lizzie, with not quite a steady hand, poured the wine, conscious all the time of Gregory's eyes on her, the faint strains of a waltz wafted across the fields on the still, frosty air, and entered the cosy room.

"Oh, listen," Lizzie said, a drop of wine falling on the scrubbed table. The drop shone like a ruby jewel.

Gregory dabbed up the drop with his finger. "I'm sorry you're missin' the social, Lizzie. Do you like to dance?"

Lizzie laughed self-consciously. "I've not had much chance, Gregory, but I'll admit it, I do like a waltz." She stuck the cork back in the bottle and slid a glass across to him.

Gregory ignored the glass; instead he stood and bowed to her. "Would you honour me by dancing this Christmas waltz, Mrs. Crellin?"

A trite retort rose to Lizzie's lips, but meeting the look in Gregory's eyes she held it back. How could she have imagined that a business arrangement would suit this decent, kindly little man? He had more depths than she had ever dreamed of. "There's not space here to dance," she said shyly, but laughing, so that in the lamplight Gregory saw her as the girl she'd been not so very long ago.

"No," he agreed. "Come along, Lizzie dear; let's dance in the farmyard, before the music stops."

9

"But I've got my overall on, Gregory, an' I'm still in my gumboots," Lizzie protested.

Gregory merely smiled and took her hand. He led her outside, where he held her as carefully within his arms as though she was wearing her finest evening dress and dainty, dancing shoes.

"You've not given me an answer," he murmured after they'd done the rounds of the cobbled farmyard several times and Lizzie was beginning to feel dizzy.

"I'll be pleased to be your wife, Gregory," Lizzie gasped, "but there's to be no talk of livin' anywhere but here. If you're to be my husband, then this is where we'll stay."

"That'll be grand," Gregory smiled and whirled her round faster. "Can I kiss you now, Lizzie?"

Lizzie, suddenly overwhelmed by the realisation that she was now an affianced woman, nodded eagerly. "But don't be takin' too long about it, Gregory," she whispered, wishing she felt more romantic, but it was so long since she'd been in practice. "The soles of these gumboots are near worn through an' my feet are fair perishin'."

AFTER THE STORM

Tholt-y-will

During the night of January 8th 2005 the Isle of Man was struck by a severe storm.

The resultant damage affected the whole island; chimneys and roofs were blown off, sheds and fences were swept from their foundations, walls and greenhouses collapsed. The north of the Island was especially badly affected.

The most costly damage was the hundreds of ancient trees torn from the ground; glens and plantations island-wide were closed for months for felled timber to be cleared and damaged paths repaired.

It will take many years to redress the havoc of that one terrifying storm. Magnificent mature trees, familiar friends to generations, were reduced to split timber, their roots wrenched from the earth as though by giant hands.

Tholt-y-will is a special place, vibrant with atmosphere from times past, with its ruined tholtans, desolate outbuildings and acres and acres of woodland. It is an area that resounds with the voices of long dead people and forgotten histories.

My brother Jack has always been practical – at the age of three he dismantled toy cars to see how they worked – on his fourth birthday he was given a miniature wood work set, complete with saw and hatchet. These tools determined his future for now he is a forest ranger living deep in Tholt-y-will, a magical place where I stay on my infrequent visits to the Isle of Man.

As well as being practical Jack has always been independent and totally self-sufficient. When he phoned one evening to say that he needed my help I was perturbed. Luckily I had a few days leave due. I booked a flight and packed books rather than an extra saw, assuming that the help Jack needed must be more in my line than his. On a gusty March morning as the flight from Gatwick swept down to Ronaldsway Airport and I glimpsed the spur of Langness and the gleam of Derbyhaven Bay I felt my usual fierce homecoming pang. I wished I could find a satisfying job that would keep me on the island forever.

As I stepped from the plane a bouquet of nostalgic scents refreshed my city-silted lungs, the clean tang of bracken and gorse from the mountains and a brine rich smell of the sea. I couldn't help beaming as I hurried to the terminal where I spotted Jack before he saw me. My little brother, who now towers over me, looked fit though tense. My anxiety deepened. As soon as I'd collected my bag I rushed to him.

"Great to see you, Kirsten, thanks for coming so quickly." Jack's lung crushing embrace took me aback. My brother's hugs were usually reserved for his favourite forest trees.

"Hey up, let me breathe. What's wrong?"

"Nothing, well, not much, now that you've come. Let's go. I can't talk here, with all these *folk* about." His frown of distaste, as though people were an alien species, made me smile. Jack has always preferred the company of trees to humans and I don't suppose that will ever change. As he took my case I thanked my lucky stars that he still cared for me. He was a one-off, my brother, and I loved him dearly, though as I clambered into his mud spattered jeep, not an easy manoeuvre owing to heeled shoes and a tight skirt, I did wish he might somctime buy a more civilised vehicle. .

"We'll drive a bit, and then I'll explain," Jack said brusquely, revving the engine. "You'll not believe me, I hardly believe it myself, but…" he flung me a look as we swung out of the car park. "Oh Kirst, it's good to see you."

I smiled and held tight to my laptop, from which I'm rarely parted. We juddered through the village of Ballasalla and took the turning towards the north of the island. I resigned myself to an uncomfortable, noisy ride. Jack's jeep should be in a museum, or scrapheap. All that can be said about it is that it goes. Considering the terrain it covers this is a miracle in itself, but some miracles I could live without. At the treacherous corner known as the Blackboards I slid from my seat, despite the sagging seat belt, as the vehicle turned abruptly off the main road. Struggling against gravity I smelled wild garlic and pictured the gleaming leaves of Ramsons edging the road past the Fairy Bridge and wished we'd gone that way. But it was too late for wishing. We swept downhill, bumped over a bridge and rattled up the other side. By this time Jack was looking less tense and his foot less heavy on the accelerator, allowing me to glimpse early primroses, wood anemones and pennywort dotting the high-grassed hedges lining the way. At a bend I twisted my neck to spy a last look at Langness and the sea. But then I had to swing quickly to the front again to keep my balance. At the foot of a long slope where sticky budded sycamores hung over the road Jack signalled a right turn. "I know where we're going," I crowed delightedly, holding on with tight knuckles as the jeep swerved.

"So you should," Jack grinned.

He was still smiling when he pulled up and leapt out. The cove of Port Grenaugh had been a favourite family picnic spot when we were young.

"I thought here'd be just right for elevenses. Come on." Jack grabbed a rucksack from under his seat, swung it onto his shoulder and set off.

I gaped at the track he was heading for. "Jack! My shoes! I'm not dressed for mud!"

"Too bad," he chortled. "You should be."

I jumped from the jeep. "Have a heart," I wailed as I tip toed towards him, "give me a hand, I don't want to land flat on my face." I was still clutching my laptop and bag. I could have left them in the jeep, but in my head I was still in England, where only an idiot leaves things in an unlocked vehicle.

"Feeble, that's what you are, Kirsten Corkhill," Jack chuckled, hauling me bodily up the slope. "To think I called on you for help. Here, come on, over this stile. Right, this'll do. I'll take off my coat. You can sit on it, seeing as you've got on that flighty suit."

I bit my lip and lowered myself gingerly onto the lining of his disreputable waxed jacket. My 'flighty' suit, as he called it, had cost an arm and a leg. I'd thought myself pretty smart and well up to par with my fellow business flyers. Jack has never been clothes conscious; save for making sure what he wore had pockets for knives etc. I daresay if he'd considered the matter at all Jack would have expected me to turn up in ripped jeans and parka, my daily outfit for the four years, including post grad, as an archaeology student. It was only now that I had a steady research job as well as a regular income, that I could afford and enjoy wearing stylish clothes.

Jack handed me coffee from a flask. He set his cup down after one quick swig. "Right. Now shut up and listen. O.K.?"

"O.K. bro," I saluted him, cheerfully intrigued. We had paused for our coffee break at a promontory fort named Cronk ny Merriu, *Hill of the Dead* in Manx Gaelic, an undeserving name as the place was never used for burials, it was an Iron Age and Viking period habitation site.

We were perched on grassy bank in the most glorious position overlooking the sea and the shingle beach. Pink thrift flowers densely dotted in the grass waved in the breeze alongside us, just as they would have done thousands of years before, when keen eyed invasion watchers sat on this very spot. I heaved a contented sigh, shook my head to feel the wind in my hair and closed my eyes.

"Don't, Kirsten. You've got to look at me; otherwise I'll think you're not listening."

14

I blinked my eyes open, startled by Jack's tone. As he began his tale a cloud stole across the sun. By the time he'd finished more clouds had gathered and I was shivering.

"You know I told you about the violent storm we had just after New Year?"

I nodded.

"I didn't say but I was trapped in the cottage for near two days."

"Oh Jack, that must have been terrible!"

He shrugged. "It wasn't too bad, save for thinking the roof was going to cave in while the storm was at its height. I kept in touch with the emergency services on my mobile." Jack's eyes darkened. "But when the storm was over and I finally got out I could have wept. The devastation, Kirst, it was unbelievable. The lads and I had to work night and day for near a fortnight just to get the roads clear, just in our area. The off road destruction was like something out of Armageddon. Thousands of trees had been felled and there was acres and acres of damage. There are glens and plantations that will stay closed yet for months."

Jack's eyes swung away. "While the first rush was on we were too busy to think, or worry. When the initial clear up was done I had time to concentrate on my own patch. That's when it – she - happened." Jack gave me a quick, wary glance. "That's why, well, at first…" Jack heaved a sigh, and shifted his bottom on the muddy bank. "You can imagine what it was like, Kirsten, in the aftermath. There were people underfoot everywhere. You know how it is after a disaster. Folk gather like flies on a corpse."

I winced at his blunt description.

"At first I thought the woman was just another sightseer, so I ignored her. But when I'd seen her not just a few times, but every time I went into the woods I began to wonder..." Jack took an uneasy breath.

I sipped Jack's foul coffee, my heart thumping. I'd never seen him so distressed.

"Though I hadn't taken much notice of her and she never came too close it got so as I could sense her, always on the periphery of where I was working. I'd be concentrating – sawing or felling, whatever, and she'd be there. I tried my best to ignore her, thinking she was just someone weird, but it got harder. For a start her appearance was wrong for a local. No one with any sense would be wearing the sort of dress she had on, not in mid-winter. Nor would they be accompanied by the hugest dog - a wolf hound." Jack wriggled uncomfortably. "It never barks, Kirst, or makes a sound." Jack took a breath, his eyes wide. "There can't be many wolf hounds on the Isle of Man, can there?"

"No," I shook my head. "Jack, what is this leading up to?"

"I'm trying to tell you. For God's sake, listen," he snapped.

In normal circumstances I wouldn't have let Jack speak to me like that. He was my *little* brother after all, but at the time I nodded obediently. A tic at the corner of his eye revealed his anxiety as much as his tetchy words.

"Remember we looked up the history of Tholt-y-will when I first applied for my job? In medieval times almost a third of the island was part of the King's Forest, belonging to the Lords of Mann."

I nodded.

"The Stanley Lords imported deer to stock the hunting grounds, which encompassed the entire area of Tholt-y-will."

"Yes, I remember all that."

"Oh, good," Jack's shoulders slumped. "I know this sounds utterly mind blowingly unbelievable, Kirsten, but I reckon this woman - whoever she is - or was - is from that time."

I had just swallowed a gulp of coffee, yet my mouth felt dry.

"I've been trying to come to terms with what could have happened on the night of the storm to bring her to life. It's just too ridiculous, I know, but when you lie awake for hours like I've been doing and go over and over things then all sorts of unlikely possibilities crop up. My latest idea is that she and her dog were buried under one of the felled trees. Now she's been released she's haunting me. Maybe she thinks that because I live there I'm to blame."

"Jack! You don't believe in ghosts. You never have."

My brother's bloodshot eyes gazed into mine. "I believe in this woman, Kirsten. I've seen her, as close as you are now."

"Oh Jack!" I gasped, "I don't know how to deal with something like this. Maybe she isn't a ghost," I said desperately. "Maybe she is local, a girl who fancies you, who just dresses oddly?"

Jack looked at my pitifully. "Don't be daft, Kirsten." He shook his head slowly and miserably. "Don't insult my intelligence."

I gripped his fingers, which felt icy. "Never mind, bro, I'm here now. Between us we'll sort this woman out."

He gave a shaky laugh. "Oh, Kirsten, I'm so glad you've come. I knew you'd believe me. You do believe me, don't you?"

"Of course I do. I can see you're in a state. You should have asked me sooner. Though what in heaven's name do you think I can do? Tell this phantom floozy to get lost?

Jack's breath came in a whoosh. "Yeah, maybe?" His eyes crinkled. "Thanks, sis, just hearing you speak about her makes me feel better. I've been bursting to tell someone, but I haven't dared. I didn't want my mates thinking me a nutter, and it's not the sort of problem you can take to your boss, is it? This woman is real, Kirsten. She's real and she's lovely, and I want to help her."

"I'm sure you do," I said, my heart thumping. There was a peculiar expression on Jack's face that disturbed me even more than what he'd said. He'd confided a lot, but he hadn't told all.

I'd always longed for Jack to find a good, kind-hearted woman who would love him, as he deserved. Now, judging by the furtive elation in his eyes it seemed that he had at last found her, but this wasn't how I'd envisaged his future. What good would a spirit woman do my gentle brother? Or what harm?

Tholt-y-will translates from Manx Gaelic to Hill of the Cattle Fold. Not that there are cattle nowadays amongst the thousands of trees surrounding Jack's mossy roofed shack.

"There would have been herds here once," Jack reminded me as we bumped towards our destination. "This area would have been open heath in medieval times."

"M'm?" I said, unclenching my teeth. The drive up the storm-wrecked track had been brain shakingly uncomfortable.

"When was it re-forested?"

"Seventeenth and early eighteenth centuries, when wealthy merchants and the Manx Government decided to replant their lands with a variety of trees, some quite exotic, though not many of those special plantings survived. The indigenous timber would have all but disappeared by the 1600s, used for fuel and building. There might have been a few ancient oaks still standing, oh, and hollies. *Ilex* is a great survivor." Jack switched off the engine and jumped out.

"Goodness!" I shook my head wonderingly.

"What?"

"There's not a sound!"

Jack hefted my case and steadied me as I jumped down. "Rubbish. I can hear collared doves, a chaffinch - sheep and," – he raised an ear – "a tractor in a field above the dam."

"You're joking. It's so quiet my ears hurt."

"Townee!" Jack grinned and unlatched the door.

Before I went into the cottage I glanced into the gloomy depths of the woodland only metres away. It looked creepy. I hoped I wasn't going to regret coming to my brother's rescue. I'm a bright lights girl nowadays. It's months since I saw a starry sky or tried to sleep without the noise of traffic and drunks outside my flat.

"It's not luxurious," Jack showed me into the tiny spare room. A quilt, bright with zigzags of colour lay on the bed.

"That's new, in your honour," he grinned. "I'll put the kettle on. Sort yourself out. There's hanging space in the cupboard."

I changed quickly into jeans and jumper. Jack's harping on about this phantom girl on the way back had disturbed me. It was clear that he had become obsessed with her. I couldn't honestly take in what he'd told me as the truth, but I knew Jack. If he said he'd seen this woman, he had. Where did that leave me? I wasn't much good at sorting out real life situations, let alone paranormal ones.

Hot tea, fat cheese sandwiches and chocolate biscuits restored my optimism, as well as the sight of Jack's crammed store cupboard. He wasn't prepared to starve himself, that was one comfort.

"You'll come with me this afternoon, Kirst, won't you? I can't afford to get behind. There's a mass to deal with still. It's going to take months."

"Of course," I said through a mouthful of biscuit. Having seen for myself the extent of the devastation as we'd driven from the mountain road I wanted to do whatever I could to help. We'd pulled into a lay-by on the sheep scattered slopes of Snaefell Mountain. Looking across the valley, where the woodland canopy had formerly been close packed and perfect, there was now a mish mash of felled trunks, the roof of Jack's cottage an indistinct spec of ochre amongst the carnage. As the jeep crossed the valley floor and negotiated the track to the cottage Jack had listed plantations where things were even worse.

I felt mounting guilt. "Why on earth didn't you tell me how serious the storm was? You must have been going through hell these last two months."

"What could you have done, Kirsten? I've coped."

Jack spoke airily but as he picked up his mug I saw his hand tremble. I felt a chill inside. I crammed another biscuit into my mouth hoping the chocolate might make me brave. I had an uneasy feeling I might need to be.

"We can't clear the destruction," Jack said as we set out moments later. "The eco-structure would go haywire, so most of the felled wood will be left to decay, providing habitat, food and shelter."

"What about rot like Dutch Elm disease?"

Jack sighed. "I try not to think of it. I just keep on doing what I can to sort the mess."

I stayed close to Jack as we walked silently over the rust coloured carpet of pine needles. Even with so many trees felled the forest was still a gloomy, creepy place. Jack was holding his chain saw and I had two visored helmets. "Well, I'm here now," I said, swinging the helmets. "I'll do whatever you want."

"Right!" Jack responded light heartedly, "you'll take first go with the chainsaw then?"

"Why not?" I pulled on a helmet, playing up to his banter. It was better than looking between the tree trunks and imagining ghosts.

"Maybe next time," Jack laughed, and then his cheerful expression fled as he prepared to work.

The next hour was fascinating. To watch any expert in their chosen field is a joy. Jack was utterly confident, utterly careful, and utterly competent. I found a convenient tree stump, a conifer with just enough girth to support my bottom and sat absorbed.

The trees that Jack had decided would need his attention already had an 'X' etched into their trunks. As there seemed to be dozens of these in the near vicinity it seemed Jack would have an endless task just getting through the work in this small area. Yet after a while he pointed out differences and I understood the need to cut down or lop some trees more urgently than others.

While he worked my mind wandered, and I felt the peace of the place calm me, despite the roaring chain saw. As we were within sight of the cottage I felt reasonably relaxed, though when Jack started to look around edgily as if he was waiting for something between each sawing bout it wasn't long before I got twitchy too, though I tried to remain calm, as I'd already begun to wonder whether Jack's visions were a result of his solitary state and his imagination. Maybe the phantom woman was actually a figment of desire, provoked by stress?

Anyhow, time passed and nothing happened, I grew easier in my mind, pretty certain that as long as I was present nothing would happen either.

So that when the buzzing chain saw in Jack's hand suddenly paused from cutting into a gashed beech tree and he stared fixedly beyond me, for a moment I wondered what was going on.

"There!" He murmured his voice low. "Can you see her?"

I swung round, but could see nothing, yet Jack's eyes were riveted, his face ashen, the chainsaw trembling in his hands, until he lowered it.

I peered dementedly. All I could see was a rotten tree trunk and a few leaves swirling in mid-air. "No I can't. Is she really there?"

"Yes, oh yes!"

I felt helpless, the usual frustration of the unseeing person. I've worked on a few digs where uncanny sightings have occurred while I remained unaware. Rationally I feel relieved not to be burdened by psychic perception. As an archaeologist it could be a distinct disadvantage. But on this occasion I wished otherwise.

Jack exhaled sharply. "N-no, she's gone." He swung round. "Maybe she doesn't like you being with me."

"Maybe not," I smiled, trying to infuse reassurance into my look. Jack shrugged off his fright and resumed working with the sober concentration of a man who knows his dangerous job inside out and

20

never, ever takes risks. As usual, after being with my brother for only a short time I was full of admiration for his dedication, and his self-control. That one brief sighting had shaken me up. Jack had been undergoing such experiences for weeks. I had an inkling that in his shoes I would have chickened out long ago and found another job.

When Jack moved to another part of the forest I selected another tree stump, a beech, this time, next to a budding wood sorrel. I gazed above at the skimpy canopy, I inspected a family of woodlice that were creeping about near my feet and I tried not to worry while wishing I could do something constructive, but as Jack kept looking towards me and half smiling I hoped he was at least gaining comfort from my presence.

By the time the shadows were lengthening and I was feeling more than a little peckish he allowed me to help him stack the logs he'd cut. They were piled haphazardly, so that as they rotted they would provide support for birds and wildlife.

"There," he said at last, wiping his forehead. "Time for supper?"

"Oh, please. My legs and arms are like jelly."

"You're out of condition," Jack joshed me.

"I know," I panted, "nowadays I work more at my pc than with a trowel."

Jack said something else and I answered, but both of us were weary and from the way his gaze kept darting from side to side, I could tell that he was more preoccupied with his spectral woman than by anything I might say, so I kept quiet. My muscles were aching, and so was my brain. How on earth, though in this case that was an inappropriate expression, was I going to help Jack?

After supper we talked of family and times past. Our parents had moved off island when we were in our teens. Jack had stayed, apprenticed to a woodsman, lodging with their family until he qualified to take on this job. I'd known that he would never leave the Isle of Man. Jack loves the land of our birth with a passion. He understands my need though, to explore a wider world, and he hopes, as I do, that one day I will return to Ellan Vannin, the cherished Manx name for our island home.

21

It was getting late and I could see that Jack was tired. I wasn't. I often get a late evening spurt of energy. I felt restless. I needed to work through this problem. I wondered how to start.

"Draw her," I said suddenly, handing him a notebook and pencil. "Give me some detail to work from."

"I can't draw," Jack protested, yawning.

"Rot! You draw plants and trees brilliantly, so you can surely make a rough sketch of this woman. Please, Jack, I need to know what she looks like."

Reluctantly Jack took the pad.

I gazed over his shoulder as he laboriously wielded the pencil. "No, you're not much of an artist. M'm, that's better. Oh." My light heartedness fled, my insides tightened as Jack's pencil sketched in more and more detail.

"She's in medieval dress all right. Mid 16th century I'd say, and yes, that is a wolf hound." I went to Jack's bookcase, which was stuffed with local history books as well as every type of treatise on wood and woodland management. "You've not spoken to anyone about her, you said?"

"My mates would think I was barking."

"Maybe you are," I agreed with sisterly affection. "Now, why don't you have an early night and leave me to these, and my lap-top. O.K.?"

Jack yawned. "Yeah, I might. I feel done in." He got up and stretched. "G'night, Kirst." He gave my hair a ruffle, a thing he'd done since childhood and which meant more to both of us than any hug or kiss, and slipped out. I gazed after him, my eyes moist. My little brother, who I'd always admired, and upon whom I'd always relied, looked grey, drawn and older than his years. Drat this phantom woman, bothering him when he had quite enough to cope with in the physical world.

I gave a grumbling sigh, picked up the sketch Jack had made, and set to work.

I looked up all the references I could find relating to the Lord's deer park and made copious notes, both from books and from my laptop, though I wasn't sure what use they'd be. Due to the untimely

22

death of Ferdinand Stanley, the 5th Earl of Derby in 1594 there was an Interregnum, with no resident Lord of Mann until 1612. During this period Queen Elizabeth assumed the Lordship title. The governance of the island during this period was shared by various officials, including one whose name caught my fancy immediately, though I had no idea why; Cuthbert Holmewood, a man of lusty appetites, for both women and hunting, I gathered, from a guardedly worded description in a British Library text. I scrolled on through reams of mostly uninteresting details of medieval rule in Mann and had just spotted an interesting mention of a hunting lodge in a 'mountainy' area when I felt a rush of cold air, like a draught from an open door. My loose pages of notes rustled and I swung round, thinking Jack was behind me.

"Jack?" The room was empty. I leapt to the door and peered into the tiny lobby. The front door, which was the only entry into the house, was still bolted, yet the chill air still hung about me and my papers stirred and rustled eerily.

I clicked off my laptop and scurried to bed. Expecting to lie awake, shivering with terror, almost as soon as I closed my eyes I fell into a dreamless sleep.

Next morning brought sunshine, a cooked breakfast and rationality. I gathered my notes and showed them to Jack.

"I wonder whether your woman was one of this Cuthbert Holmewood's lovers. Maybe she died here in a hunting accident."

"But wouldn't she be buried in church ground?" He said, frowning. "I thought they were keen on that sort of thing in medieval times."

"Not if she was an illicit courtesan and there was something fishy about her death."

"You've too much imagination, Kirsten. They wouldn't bury her dog with her, would they?"

I hesitated, not wanting to dispel Jack's enviably naïve view of mankind, present and past. "I don't know," I shrugged.

"O.K. but why's she haunting me?"

"Well, obviously she's been disturbed by the storm. Have you any particularly ancient trees in this vicinity? That have been storm damaged, I mean?"

"No. Oh, yeah, there's one that's a bit special. A twin trunked oak, it split, though one trunk's still undamaged."

I looked at the rough sketch Jack had drawn the night before. The image blurred before my gaze. I was warm, full of toast and a cheerful March sun was beaming through the window. "Can't we go for a drive to a nice open beach?" I asked hopefully. "I'm scared."

Jack laid a calloused hand on mine. "So am I, Kirsten. "I'll have to leave here unless I can get this sorted. I'm relying on you."

Isn't this just what any sister wants to hear? Well, not exactly, but it boosted my ego.

"Come on. Lets recce."

This time I led the way, shivering a bit, for although the sun was bright it was still chilly. As we tramped across the patch of sunlit open ground to the forest, where bluebells were thrusting their shiny leaves into view and scatters of primroses were in early bud, I tried to imagine myself into this woman's skin. Entering the tree canopy I took Jack's hand. "Think of her," I ordered, "think hard and perhaps she will show herself."

We walked for maybe ten minutes, deep into the green gloom, stepping over fallen trees, avoiding uprooted stumps, aware of the scents of rot and regrowth, the subdued call of wood pigeons and the rustle and cheep of nesting birds who'd taken advantage of the storm destruction to relocate. Between the trees, far away, I caught a glitter of the Sulby dam. I wished I were sitting beside it in the sunshine.

Jack came to a sudden halt. "It's no use, Kirsten. She only appears when I'm working. This is a waste of time. Let's go back. I've got paperwork to catch up on."

We retraced our steps. I started telling Jack about my latest project, a survey of Civil War sites that I've been involved with for the past six months and which I find fascinating. We were within sight of the clearing in which the cottage stood; in fact I was staring towards the bluebell leaves we'd passed earlier, when Jack's hand tightened on my arm. "She's there, Kirsten, not more than twenty feet ahead. Leaning against that beech. The dog's at her feet."

Jack stopped in his tracks. I yanked him on. "Keep your eyes on her. How does she look? What's her body language?"

Jack's voice was hoarse, his hand trembling on my arm. "Her shoulders are slumped. She looks tired. Wait, she's looking up. Her eyes are – "

His arm dropped. "Oh, Kirst, she's gone."

We reached the slim beech tree she'd been leaning against. Jack thumped it irritably. "What's she doing this for, Kirsten? Why me?"

I put arm around him. "Take it easy, Jack. You were going to say something about her eyes. What?"

Jack frowned. "She looked," he bunched his fists helplessly. "Oh – I don't know – I don't know how to express it - I'm no good with words."

"Try," I prompted. "Please."

"She looked – imploring. Is that what I mean – you know, wanting something?"

I gripped his hand. "Wanting – beseeching. But wanting what?" I inspected the sapling she'd been leaning against. "Well, this looks fine, but what about that one over there, good heaven's – it's huge. Is that the split oak you mentioned?"

"Yes, but it's safe, I tell you. I've dealt with it. I did it soon after the storm."

"Are you sure?"

"Yes, I am. Look, I sawed through here where it was shattered. It had only a minor amount of rot, but this other trunk is absolutely sound." Jack thumped the grainy bark of the oak reassuringly. "You'll probably stand for another hundred years, won't you, old man."

We both gazed at the splendid tree trunk soaring above us, the branches mostly bare, only a few tipped by tiny buds.

"Maybe it's not this one then," I said, conscious of disappointment but trying to muster optimism. For goodness sake, I'd only been here twenty-four hours. It was unlikely I'd sort the matter out so soon. I pushed to the back of my mind a more realistic outcome; that I'd never sort it at all.

"Let's go back then," I said, clasping Jack's hand like we used to do when we were little. We strolled towards the cottage, which

25

looked safe and homely now that the sun was higher. I gazed at the shabby front door, at the crumbling stone of the cottage walls and how they seemed almost to merge into a fern studded rocky bank, where a cluster of scrawny primroses were growing in an oddly symmetrical arrangement. A curious sensation made me stop short. Maybe it was because I was tense that I saw something I'd never seen before, a series of faint contours, which in archaeological terms meant only one thing.

"Goodness!" I hurried towards the bank, got down on my knees and with my fingers felt the ridge along which the primroses had seeded, along with a cluster of tiny saxifrage. "Jack, look, have ever you noticed? I reckon there was another building here, a larger structure, if this is a foundation line, and I'm almost sure it is."

"Go on, surely that's natural? There were no other buildings in this wood except the corn mill and the Forester's Lodge and I know where the remains of those are."

"Well this is definitely a foundation line." I gazed up at Jack excitedly. "What if the Lord of Mann's hunting lodge was originally situated here?"

My brother gaped at me with undisguised horror. "What if it was? I don't want teams of archaeologists digging me up. Then I really would have to leave."

"You want my help, don't you? You want to solve the problem of this ghost?"

"She's not a problem," Jack retorted. "She's well, yeah, O.K. maybe she is a problem." He shrugged dejectedly. "Come on. I need a caffeine boost. Let's get inside."

Jack made coffee and I tried to sort everything out in my head. This restless spirit had to be showing herself for some reason. She was appearing to Jack even when I was present. Was that significant? I was only a visitor, of course. Though I was his sister and no doubt gave off similar vibes it was Jack who looked after the woodland and cared passionately about it. His trees were his family; they were precious, if anything happened to one of them…

A bell tinkled in the deep recesses of my mind.

"Drat, I forgot to get torch batteries when I picked you up. I'll have to get some from Sulby village. Do you want to come?

I frowned. "I'd like to, but I think I'll stay here. You won't be long?"

"'Bout half an hour."

"Right. I'll sit outside and think."

Jack swigged his coffee and grabbed his keys. "Don't strain yourself," he grinned, pulling the door to, though not so quickly that I missed seeing his face stiffen with anxiety again, which immediately made me panic. After a lifetime of dogged independence Jack had been impelled to ask me for help, but what if I couldn't help, ever?

As the sound of Jack's jeep rattling down the track faded I carried an old waterproof and a couple of cushions outside. I settled myself against the wall of the cottage and closed my eyes. Though a chill breeze competed with the fitful sunshine, it was pleasant there. A bee buzzed past, close to my nose, startling me. He was on the pollen trail early, I thought, blinkingly following his progress, though I soon lost sight of him against a clump of last year's bracken. Faint rustlings came from a yellow budded gorse bush on the nearby bank; a tiny bird tweeted and swooped past me a couple of times. It might have been a wren. Jack would have known. I thought myself back through the centuries, to when this area might have been the hub of a busy hunting scene, lively with servants preparing for a hunting party; beds to be aired, provisions to be cooked, animals to be killed to serve at table.

I must have dozed because the next thing I recall is blinking my eyes open and finding myself in shadow. I looked up crossly, wriggling my way from the dark stripe lying over the cottage and me. My eyes began to droop again, when the significance of the shadow struck me. I leapt dizzily to my feet.

Bleary eyed I raced beneath the tree canopy, leaping over fallen logs and darting around shattered spruce trunks. After the brilliant sunlight the gloom was initially near impenetrable. I kept my eyes ahead but every so often I glanced back. I had to trace the long shadow to its source.

I was onto something, I sensed it; excited dread spurred me on, making me exhilarated, yet shaky. The deeper I plunged into the gloom the more intensely I felt a mounting nervousness. This was not an entirely new feeling. Once I'd been skiing in an avalanche region when a similar feeling of danger enveloped me. Because I had responded immediately I escaped being swept away, while other skiers died. Some people belittle intuition, or call it luck. I would never be so crass.

Following the long shadow led me circuitously, but unsurprisingly, to the ancient forked oak, its damaged trunk neatly cut above the roots, the other trunk soaring upwards. I laid both hands on the tree and leaned my cheek against it.

With my eyes closed I heard a painfully beating heart. Was it my heart I was listening to or...?

"Kirsten, what *are* you doing? You shouldn't have come in here on your own."

Now my heart really hammered. I'd not heard Jack's footsteps. I'd been so absorbed I hadn't even heard his jeep driving up the track. I was trembling, yet buoyed up and joyful. I grabbed his hand. "Jack! I had to come. I've worked it out, I'm sure. Quickly, look."

I dragged him a few yards distant. "Look up there. Follow the tree's shadow. It's almost mid-day and the trunk is like the finger on a sundial, the shadow lying plumb across your cottage." I squeezed his fingers, willing him to understand. "That is how the tree would lie if it fell. I'm sure that's what your phantom woman is trying to tell you. She's concerned for you, Jack. She knows the oak is dangerous. She wants you to cut it down."

Jack gave me a comically despairing look. "Who's the expert, Kirsten?" he grinned, and then his face changed, his cheeks paled and his eyes swivelled past me.

"You can see her, can't you?"

"Oh Kirsten, what does she want?"

"Quick, put your mark on the trunk. You've got your knife haven't you?"

"But..."

"Do it! If it isn't necessary you're not committed. But if it is..."

Jack gazed at me appealingly, confusedly, desperately. Then he whipped out his knife and slashed a hasty 'X' on the bark of the soaring oak.

28

"Now what? How does she look?"

"Kirsten, you're right! She's smiling; she's reaching out," his fingers trembled as he moved swiftly, holding out his own hand. The sight of this made the hairs on the back of my neck stand on end. What if he touched her, what if…?

"No," Jack's hand dropped, "She's stroking the hound," a weird sad smile lit his face. "She's…" he swung round, grey faced once more. "She's gone."

Jack slid his razor sharp knife back in its sheath. "I can't believe that tree's rotten. It just can't be."

I grabbed his hand. "Come on, we're getting your chain saw. We'll get this trunk down and with luck you won't see your lady friend again."

Jack gave that smile again and I had to look away, for behind his relief I glimpsed a bereft sadness. My heart went out to him. How would I feel if I'd met the man of my dreams, yet I could never hold him in my arms?

Less than an hour later the oak fell with a crash that shook the forest. For long moments shards of wood and splinters rained on us. Jack had insisted I wear a helmet and ear protectors and I was glad of them.

My brother's face was paler than the split trunk as we inspected the debris. "You were right, Kirsten. The tree was rotten. Rotten all through, and I couldn't tell. Why? I should have known!"

I nodded, and shivered, shock getting to me. .

Jack put his arm around my shoulders. "At any time it might have fallen on the cottage. In the next gale, that would have been that." He pulled me to him. "I'd never have woken up, Kirst. I'd have been here for ever."

"That's what she was trying to tell you, Jack," I said as he held me. "She cared. Who knows how, but she cared." I wanted to comfort Jack, I felt so sorry for him.

"I suppose I'll never see her again." he turned away, looking towards the cottage, his face bleak, then imperceptibly his expression changed, he smiled and reached out. A shiver ran through me. I knew he could see her, and still I could see nothing.

"She's there," he said hoarsely, moving slowly, smiling all the while, his hand reaching further and further – then his face fell and his hand dropped. "She's fading, Kirsten. She's fading... and gone. For good, do you think?"

"Maybe," with my foot I was shovelling loose earth into the void left by the wrenched out tree roots, under which I could see ancient bones, human and canine. My archaeological knowledge made recognition instantaneous, but I wanted to hide this sad debris from Jack. Let him remember his lady as young, beautiful and alive, albeit in spectral form.

A week later, I left Jack, restored more or less to his former self. As the plane soared into the sky and I looked down upon the airport car park and the tiny figure that was my brother, waving, I wondered what the future might hold for him; this kindly, gentle man who lived his life so much in tune with his environment that the spirits of the past felt obliged to protect him.

I vowed to visit Jack more often. Clearly he was very special. As I cradled my laptop I reflected humbly that although my qualifications enabled me to chase around the globe in pursuit of my career my brother Jack, in his little forest home, on our precious island, had achieved a harmony with nature, past and present, to which I could never even hope to aspire.

Extract from diary, 2006.

Today I was studying a Manx Assize book from 1590. An offence concerning a Lezayre land owner, Cuthburt Holmewood, caught my eye, accused of 'brutally putting to death a woman and hound.' After a summary trial at Peel Castle Holmewood was exonerated. Upon his release, however, an unknown assailant, believed to be the woman's lover, waylaid Holmewood and knifed him to death. This assailant, a woodsman, was subsequently hanged.
I photocopied this item to send to Jack, but then I thought again and tore it up. Jack has a proper girlfriend now; a lovely 21st century woman.

ALL THIS AND CRÈME BRULEE

Douglas

Magazine stories require varying styles depending on their readership. This makes writing challenging, but fun, if one can find the right voice. This story, which first appeared in 'Woman's Weekly,' is based on my memories of Douglas in the nineteen fifties and sixties, the heyday of the Manx boarding house, before such establishments routinely became known as 'guest houses'.

At that time I lived near Broadway and Hutchinson Square, a typical boarding house district, lively with tourists all summer, as well as itinerant seasonal staff, many of whom flitted at whim from one business to the next as tiffs inevitably occurred.

The visitors that poured in their thousands from the Steam Packet ships in those days were unconcerned about staff upheavals and behind the scene dramas. As long as their meals were tasty and the beds comfortable they were out of doors soon after breakfast, revelling in all that was available in this glamorous resort, and determined to fill each precious moment with new experiences. Each afternoon the Villa Marina and Palace Gardens were packed for the bathing beauty competitions and band concerts; the sands were crowded, the ice cream kiosks and deck chair sellers were always busy. When night fell and the twinkling promenade lights were lit a tangible air of romance hung over the entire bay, from Douglas Head to White City,

Burdened by the wearisome routine tasks of cooking, cleaning and always being on call, boarding house keepers sometimes dreamed too, even as they prepared another morning's onslaught of 'the full English.' Occasionally these romantic dreams came true.

Luminous foamy waves crashed at the sea's edge as I hurried across the promenade at Broadway. My heart thumped, my head felt light, my feet twitched. The Central Hotel was disgorging drinkers; otherwise I would have kicked through the litter in the gutter as I skipped my way up the hill past the Villa to Derby Square.

My hand shook as I inserted my key. The lounge lights were still on, some of my B & B guests must still be about. I tiptoed along the hall and slipped through the door marked Private.

Safely out of public view I twirled and threw my arms in the air. "I'm in love, I'm in love, I'm in love!"

"And where do you think you've been?" My daughter Trisha, her expression almost as sharp as the bacon scissors she was clutching, stepped out of the kitchen while I was mid-twirl.

"It's past eleven. You didn't say you were going out."

"It's only just past."

"I was worried sick. For goodness' sake, why didn't you say before you sloped off?"

"Sorry," I sighed, suppressing a grin. It's weird, when your daughter tells you off.

"Oh, you're impossible." Trisha stamped back into the kitchen.

"Shall I help?" I leaned dreamily against the door jamb. Trisha slid a tray of bacon, neatly trimmed, into the fridge. Eggs were piled in a bowl nearby; the magnetic notepad listed next morning's menu: Twenty full breakfasts, two scrambled, one boiled, two kippers.

"I've done it all. Get to bed. You'll have to be up at six."

"Oh. G'night." I scuttled away. I'd forgotten that two of my visitors were catching the early ferry. I sped up the stairs, alert as ever for guestly sounds.

"Safe," I breathed, reaching my attic bedroom and kicking off my sandals. The sand between my toes felt scratchily wicked. I closed my eyes. My head still pounded, though not with alcohol. We'd only had two half pint shandies, Alec would be working at dawn and he wasn't a man to take risks.

Though he's risky enough for me,' I thought, winding myself in the duvet in an effort to recapture the wonderful sensation of being wrapped in his strong arms.

"What a night, what a night," I murmured, letting my eyelids fall shut, the better to remember. In moments I was asleep, adrift on a warm current of Alec filled dreams. Some hours later I wakened, sweating, trapped in the duvet and with a splitting headache.

I unwrapped myself, threw off my clothes and opened the window, glimpsing a snapshot view of glittering sea and moon before falling back into my dreams, until the alarm bellowed at me at six am.

Twenty five breakfasts later I was returning to a sort of reality. A reality in which the kitchen mirror revealed I was no picture, with my whey coloured face and listless dishcloth hair. Funny, inside I still felt stunning.

After doing the washing up, I nibbled toast and drank three cups of tea while Millie, my reliable summer help, filled me in on the latest drama in her life.

"Honestly, Bel, he had that look in his eye. "Darren," I said, 'don't you try to pull the wool over me. I'm no kid.'"

I nodded and nodded again. Listening to Millie gave me space to mull over my own thoughts, though wild horses wouldn't have dragged them out of me. Unlike Millie, I like to hug things to my chest.

And these thoughts warmed me more than any amount of hot tea. Alec's face, close to mine, the stars, glimpsed briefly between kisses. Had it really happened? Had he really said what I remembered he'd said? Had he really meant it?

And when I got home, had Trisha really been cross with me? Or just worried? She'd hardly said a word before leaving for work, but then I'd been dozily frying eggs and bacon and would barely have noticed if she had.

I should have told her, though, that I was going to meet Alec, instead of slipping out as if I was ashamed of bringing him home.

I wasn't ashamed. Just a bit…well, anxious, perhaps. In case Trisha didn't like him. In case, somehow, she put him off me. Made him see what I was to her – OK as a mum, but not the most capable person in the world. A bit soft...

I flushed. I was a bit soft. Well, it's hardly a crime, is it, not to be able to watch scary things on TV or upsetting hospital programmes?

But I'm quite good as a B & B landlady as long as I don't have to talk to the guests too much. And I can fry a complete English breakfast with my eyes closed. Just as well, really…

The phone's sudden ring made me jump and spill my tea.

"Shall I get it? My, you don't look too good this morning. That time of the month, is it?" Millie grabbed the phone before I had time to mop ineffectually at the tea drips.

"It's for you," Millie said. "I'll get on upstairs, shall I?" She winked broadly as she walked away.

My heart began to beat like a steam hammer. "Hello?"

"Hi, you?"

The soft, loving tone made shivers run down my spine. My insides jellied. "Alec."

"I just had to ring you, Bel. To hear your voice."

"Did you?" I was beaming now, hot tingles vibrating under my ribs.

"I'll be round your way soon. Will you be in?"

"Probably. Maybe. Yes." Well, my visit to Shoprite could easily be postponed.

"Try to be in, my love. Otherwise I'll see you tonight?"

"Yes…"

"Are you all right, Bel? You sound sort of distant."

"I'm in love," I whispered, and revelled in the throaty laugh that came through the receiver.

"Yes, right." Alec's voice became brisk and I was aware of noise and ribaldry in the background. "I must go, lover. See you later."

The line went dead. I sighed, a heavy wonderful sigh and floated upstairs. Not even the thought of my share of twenty – odd beds and associated en-suite bathrooms dented my euphoria.

Only a guilty twinge as I peeped into Trisha's immaculately tidy room gave me pause for thought. If this was the real thing, how would it all pan out? I loved my daughter, but I loved Alec too.

I pulled sheets and duvet from the bed. Trisha had years and years ahead of her. My shelf-life was limited. I hadn't time to waste. I'd been seriously middle aged until the day when Alec stepped onto my doorstep, a registered letter in his hands.

He wasn't a complete stranger. We'd known each other in our teens. We'd fallen into an easy gossip, which he'd disrupted by asking me out for a drink. I'd been astonished, thought twice about it, and then said yes.

Trisha looked disapproving when I told her, as though I was acting out of character. I suppose I was really. I'd got used to a man-less life – how, I don't know. Now I feel young again, and loved.

But there's a crunch coming up. Sooner or later, Alec and Trisha have to meet. Suddenly my teenage romance is beginning to feel like a grown-up affair. I hope I'm woman enough to stand the pressure.

Scrubbing hand basins and changing sheets is excellent therapy. I felt quite chirpy by the time I'd finished.

Millie's cheerful chatter helped too, though I can't say that I recall much of what she said. But she did make a remark as she was leaving that struck home.

"It's good to see you lit up again, Bel," she said, sticking a cigarette between her mulberry red lips. "You've looked like a wet weekend for years. Perhaps you'll tell your Trisha to find a life now. At her age she shouldn't be tied to your apron strings."

Then she blew smoke and grinned. "Ta-ra," she said and set off up the road, her short skirt revealing more leg than I'd ever dared expose, and I can give Millie a year or two.

What did she mean? Tied to my apron strings? Often it felt more the other way round.

Trisha was thirteen when my husband Derek was killed. We'd just taken on the business. From that time on I stopped thinking of Trisha as my young daughter and more as a good friend to rely on. Trish, bless her, has never let me down.

Living here on the Isle of Man, where motorcycle races are a way of life and the racing circuit, the TT course, is known throughout the world, it's a matter of statistics that some racers will die. Yet I hadn't expected one of those statistics to be my Derek.

When his engine seized up on the first lap of a race one warm and lovely September afternoon, killing him instantly, I was devastated. It took me a long time to come to terms with his death. In fact, whether I ever have is perhaps a moot point. Sometimes I feel that Trisha has done the maturing for both of us.

Until now. Now, suddenly, I felt all woman. I raced upstairs to shower and change. Just in case. Then I made a list of what I needed at Shoprite. Though I was barely concentrating, and when the doorbell rang I found I'd written three dozen eggs twice.

"Alec!"

"Bel." I don't think Alec has ever called me Belinda, which is a pretty name, but childish, don't you think? When Alec says 'Bel' I feel grown up and beautiful.

"Hi, gorgeous," he murmured, kissing me thoroughly, much to the delight of an elderly couple who were coming downstairs.

"We just popped back for our umbrella," Mr Gibson, one of my regular summer guests, smiled.

"It looks showery," White haired, lavender scented Mrs Gibson added, slipping fragrantly past.

"I feel like a scarlet woman," I murmured as the door closed behind them.

"Good," Alec said. "Now how about coming out for a meal tonight? You and Trisha."

My throat went dry. "No, it's too soon. I don't think she'll want to come. She's very…"

Alec put his finger gently to my lips to stop me. "Ask her, Bel, please. For my sake."

What could I say?

I asked her.

"No," was the immediate reply. "Why should I?"

"He wants to get to know you. I want you to get to know him. He's so nice, Trish."

"Good," Trisha said, "but I'm not coming. I'd feel like a gooseberry."

"Please Trisha. I've never asked you to do this before." Meet a man I'm absolutely crazy about, I meant. But how could any woman say that, in all earnestness, to her own daughter?

"No, you haven't," Trisha sighed. "All right, I'll come." She gave me a long look. "Mum, are you sure what you're doing is sensible?"

As she left the room my heart sank. I just knew it would be a disastrous evening, like having a critical elder sister looking over your shoulder on a heavy date. I hoped that Alec wouldn't go right off me. And what on earth would I wear to please them both?

I compromised between middle aged mum and seaside landlady. It wasn't a success, Alec looked somewhat surprised, Trisha amused, at my unalluring navy and white spotted top and skirt.

As our dinner venue Alec had chosen one of those pubs where the helpings were lavish but the healthy options few.

Trisha looked severe as she scrutinised the menu. "Tuna salad and baked potato," she said at last.

Alec and I plumped for steak, chips and veg.

"So, you're training to be an accountant?" Alec asked.

"It's a good career," Trisha said coolly.

"She's doing very well," I said.

Alec took a sip of wine. "My dad wanted me to go into something lucrative, like a bank, when I left school, but I was desperate to get away, to taste the high life across."

"Trisha's happy here," I said, gulping red wine and hoping my face wouldn't soon match it. "She never had the hankering some get, to leave the island as soon as they've left school."

"Mum," Trisha protested, "of course I did. It's just that I knew it was out of the question. I had… responsibilities."

My mouth fell open. "You never said." Then the import of her words struck home. "For heaven's sake, Trish. I'm perfectly capable of looking after myself, you know."

Trisha tightened her lips with what I can only describe as a quirk of amusement. "Mother, as a landlady you're eminently capable. Business wise, you've got the acumen of a child of six."

37

"No, I haven't. I'm just not very good at adding up."

Alec and Trisha exchanged glances, knowing glances it seemed to me. Suddenly I felt foolish and inadequate and all the other emotions I knew I'd feel bringing them together.

I reddened, I could feel it. I glanced at Alec, wishing that he and I were sitting on the beach at Broadway again, with only the stars for company.

Then I felt guilty, so I drank some more wine. Luckily Alec changed the subject and the moment passed.

Trisha slipped off to the Ladies' when we were nearing the end of our main course and Alec laid his hand warmly on top of mine which was, by then, rather damp. "She's a nice girl, Bel, and very protective of you."

"She makes me feel so inadequate," I murmured, waiting for his denial to soothe me.

"I think you are," Alec grinned. "I think you need someone to lean on."

I tried to pull my hand away. "Well, thank you very much."

"Don't be hurt, Bel," he said, leaning over to kiss me so that I smelled his musky aftershave and shivers ran right down my legs. "I love you."

I should have stood up then, flung my napkin down and said that I didn't want, or need, to lean on any man. I'd coped well enough in the last six years since Derek died, hadn't I? I'd run my business without a single hitch. Well, excluding all that VAT fuss when I thought I might end up in prison.

I didn't say any of that, of course. Instead I pressed my hands to my middle, for I'd felt a pain, a pain that might have had something to do with the pile of chips I'd eaten along with all that steak. But no, this wasn't an over eating pain – this was an over longing pain. At last I could give up the unequal struggle of 'coping' and cede to the longed for sensation of being looked after and loved.

Trisha returned. "Mum, are you all right. You look a bit peculiar." She cast Alec a suspicious glance. "What have you been saying? She's very vulnerable, you know."

There they were again. Talking about me as though I was a fragile china dish instead of the wrong side of ten stone.

38

"I just said that I loved her," Alec explained with that touch of assurance that most postmen have, probably from dealing with mad dogs.

"Good," Trisha smiled. "She'll like that." She picked up the menu. "I think I may have a sweet. Oh look, Mum, they've got crème brulee. Your favourite. Shall I order it for you?"

I opened my mouth, and then shut it again. Yes, let them do the ordering. Let them do the talking. I didn't care. All I cared about was that a warm sort of joy was coursing through me; a joy that promised a wonderful new, man-full life.

I reached out my hand towards my glass. Trisha swiftly whipped it away. "You'll need to be up at six, remember, four guests will need early breakfast."

I shrugged. "Couldn't I have a teeny, tiny brandy?"

"No," Alec and Trisha said firmly.

I gasped. Was this conspiracy of concern really what I'd been longing for all those nights when I had only a library book to take to bed?

I giggled and kicked my shoes off under the table. Alec's look of pleased surprise when my seeking toes touched his shin was all that I could have wished for by way of an answer.

Our eyes met and we both acknowledged the fact that one day Trisha would move on to a life of her own and then, and then…

The crème brulee was wonderful too.

THE CHRISTMAS GIFT

Sulby – Douglas

One day in 1948 my six years old sister Pamela was put on the train at Ramsey to travel alone to Ballaugh, where May Corlett, our much loved Nana, would join her to travel to Douglas. Their destination was 'The Guild' – The Manx Music Festival, which has been an annual cultural highlight on the Island since the late nineteenth century.

Pam and Nana were journeying to watch the children's dance classes, at that time an extremely popular section of the Festival, held in the red velvet splendour of the Palace Theatre and adjoining annexe on Douglas Promenade.

Some years later, when we lived in Douglas, I was taken to these entrancing dance competitions and often wished I was brave enough to perform in front of an audience in that magical setting.

My sister's adventure, and how she must have felt travelling alone on the train, eventually resulted in this story which first appeared in 'The People's Friend' annual of 2006.

Hannah Corkhill waved importantly as the train drew out of Ramsey Station. Her father, Mick, gradually receded until he looked no bigger than a toy doll, and the station buildings something she could have bought from a toy shop.

Hannah tugged energetically on the thick leather strap to close the window, and then plumped back on to the cushioned seat, beaming.

She felt so full of excitement that her breakfast toast refused to settle. Here she was, on her way to Douglas, on the day before Christmas Eve!

It would have been grand to be going all that way alone. That would have been really exciting, but Grandma would be joining her at Sulby, two stops along the line. Until then, she could pretend she was a great lady, off to do her Christmas shopping in the metropolis.

With aloof deliberation, Hannah undid the ties on her hat and removed it. Mother had said to take her hat and gloves off in the train, and loosen her coat; otherwise she might feel cold when she reached Douglas. Hannah did this, bowing to right and left, just as she imagined a great lady might.

Then Hannah discarded her fine lady manner because the train had almost reached the inkpot-shaped house and she had to look out at it, crossing her fingers at the same time. If she didn't see the inkpot house on her way out of Ramsey, she always felt she might have bad luck.

She couldn't risk bad luck today. Today she was not just on a shopping trip, but on a vital mission for Daddy. It made her stomach churn pleasantly to think about it.

"Now, I shall review my finances," Hannah declared grandly. This was a phrase she'd heard Mummy say, jokingly, before she made out her shopping list.

41

Hannah pulled two purses out of her red shoulder bag. Her brown purse held her saved pocket money, and the black purse held three crisp ten-shilling notes.

She took out the notes and inspected them. They were very fine looking. In a way, Hannah thought that they were prettier than whatever she might buy with them, thought she knew that was not the sort of admission to make to a grown-up.

Hannah loved money. She gloated over each week's pocket money and was always on the lookout for dropped halfpennies.

"Look after the pennies and the pounds will look after themselves," Hannah declared, imitating Grandma and one of her favourite sayings, as she pulled the arm rest into place and sat erect against the seat back, flapping her hand regally to a herd of cows as the train steamed past.

Sometimes, she liked to pretend she was Princess Elizabeth or Margaret Rose. She wondered what the princesses were doing today and whether they were going Christmas shopping too.

Suddenly the train whistled and Hannah realised they were nearing Sulby. She quickly pulled down the window strap on the platform side.

"Grandma, Grandma," she cried as the train drew to a halt. "Here I am!"

The guard ran along the platform to ensure that Grandma got helped into the carriage.

"All right now, little girl?" He smiled, and Hannah nodded politely.

Nevertheless, when he'd hurried off to blow his whistle, she muttered under her breath. "I'm not a little girl, I'm almost nine."

"You be glad you're a little girl, Hannah. Being a big girl's not much fun. Look at my chilblains!"

Hannah looked obediently at the pink lumps on Grandma's fingers, thought she didn't think it was quite nice to display such things. Mummy often said that Grandma was only happy when she had something to moan about, but Hannah knew that Grandma could be jolly and cheerful when she liked.

Today was one of her cheerful days.

Grandma began to talk. In fact, but for a few moments when Hannah got a word in edgeways, Grandma talked non-stop all the way to Douglas.

She told Hannah who lived in each house alongside the track and when they'd moved there. She spoke about what she was going to buy, and what it had been like when she'd been a little girl. Then, she said, the Christmas trains had been so jam-packed; you could hardly get on, let alone have a carriage to themselves.

"Too many cars, today. Folks is too rich for their own good," she declared.

Hannah yawned, and then hastily covered her mouth.

"Are you sleepy? Never mind, pet. Sure as herrings is bony, Douglas will wake you up." Grandma laughed, gathering her various bags. "Why look, Hannah, it's started to snow. Now that's real Christmassy!

"We will get home, won't we Grandma?" Hannah asked anxiously.

"Of course we will, pet, though I reckon we might have a white Christmas yet. Now, get your bonnet tied and your coat fastened. My, that's a bonnie handbag. You're quite the lady."

"It's one of Mummy's old bags," Hannah confided, as they got out of the carriage where they were swept along by the rest of the good humoured passengers.

"Keep hold of my hand, Hannah, child. There's no knowing what it'll be like in Strand Street."

Hannah's insides clenched as they hurried from the station and turned along the quay. Strand Street! The main shopping thoroughfare of Douglas town; how grand it sounded.

Just how grand it was Hannah discovered when they joined the merry crowd of Christmas shoppers thronging the narrow street; bright shop windows gleamed enticingly into the far distance; festively decorated cafes and restaurants released tempting aromas of coffee and home baking.

Hannah was just thinking how long it had been since breakfast when Grandma abruptly steered her into a narrow lobby and up a steep flight of lino covered stairs.

"A trip to Douglas wouldn't start right without a pot of tea," Grandma declared, leading her to a table near a roaring fire. "I always come here before getting down to business."

"Do you?" Hannah exclaimed, surprised, and was about to enquire further when a soberly dressed waitress with a frilled white apron hurried up, her order pad at the ready.

"Tea and scones for two, please," Grandma said. She gave Hannah an indulgent glance. "And a dish of jam."

The waitress nodded and rushed off. Grandma leaned across the table.

"We'll spoil ourselves, shall we, Hannah, love?"

Hannah smiled. This was how she'd like to live all the time – warm, waited on, her purse bulging with pennies and Christmas just around the corner.

She felt a sudden pang. She hadn't thought about Mummy since she'd left home. Mummy had been feeling poorly that morning, and Auntie Jean had come to sit with her while Daddy was out.

As if reading her mind, Grandma leaned across the table. "There'll be a new little brother or sister soon, Hannah."

"I know," Hannah whispered. Another pang smote her. How would she cope with a brother or sister when she was used to being the centre of attention?

"They'll look up to you," Grandma assured her.

Hannah looked curiously at Grandma. How had she known exactly what she was thinking?

"Pot of tea for two, scones and jam." The waitress set the china and cutlery out with experienced swiftness.

"Thank you," Hannah smiled, and Grandma nodded her approval.

"The scones look good. Tuck in, Hannah, love. We've got lots to do after this. Hannah didn't need encouraging. She tucked in.

Afterwards, Hannah and Grandma visited several shops, where Grandma accumulated innumerable parcels. Hannah bought a striped tie for her father and a pretty scarf for her mother. After much deliberation she chose a pair of woolly bootees with blue ribbons for the new baby, even though Grandma had suggested that yellow might be more sensible.

Hannah was pleased with her purchases, but surprised by how much they'd cost. Her purse was almost empty.

As they emerged from the baby wear shop into the street, she pulled on Grandma's hand.

"I have to get something else, but I don't know where to get it. It's a special thing from Daddy to Mummy, you see."

"Oh yes," Grandma said. "What is this special thing?"

"They're things really, but they're private, Hannah murmured, shrugging and looking uncomfortable.

"Grandma chuckled. "Go on, tell me."

"I'll whisper," Hannah said.

Grandma put her head down. Hannah spoke a few conspiratorial words.

"Oh, them's no problem. Come along we'll get them in Tossie Cowin's. She began to hurry back the way they'd come, and then she noticed Hannah's face.

"Aw, goodness, child, you look all in. Shall we have our dinner before we finish our shopping? Would you like that?

"Yes, please, Grandma."

Meat pie and vegetables, a glass of water and a sit down, restored Hannah, though she still felt bemused by the crowds and her head had started to ache. There were so many people in Douglas. Somehow, when she'd imagined this day, it hadn't been like this at all.

As she stared around, it occurred to her that if she were a princess, life might be like this all the time. In which case, she was glad she was not a princess. She'd rather be herself, Hannah Corkhill, from Waterloo Road, Ramsey, Isle of Man.

"Now we'll get Daddy's present." Grandma winked as she counted the money for their bill, and then pushed a three penny piece across the table to put under the plate for the waitress. "You must always do that, Hannah. These girls work hard for their money."

Hannah looked at the waitresses, rushing about laden with trays, and thought how clever they looked, and how tireless.

45

"I worked as a waitress when I was young," Grandma admitted. "My feet have never been right since."

Hannah gazed at her wonderingly. Had Grandma really ever been slim enough to slip between tables like that? It seemed impossible.

The hosiery shop was quiet and rather refined. Hannah felt uncomfortable, but Grandma did the talking and soon they were looking at a selection of the most delicate nylon stockings Hannah had ever seen.

How much did Daddy give you, pet?" Grandmas asked and Hannah delved into her red bag to find the special purse with the three crisp ten-shilling notes.

She pulled out her brown purse with its few pennies, her handkerchief, a cough sweet a comb and a pencil. She felt her face getting hot. Where was the black purse?

Feeling agitated, she tipped her bag upside down on the glass counter.

The assistant, who had looked superior when they entered, began to look sympathetic, and that made Hannah feel worse.

"I must have lost it." She sniffed. "Oh, Grandma, I must have lost it."

"Well, there, there," Grandma said, looking a little put out. She felt in her own bag and found her purse and paid for a pair of sheer nylon stockings.

"I do hope the young lady finds the missing article, madam," the assistant said, as they gathered their belongings.

"So do I," Grandma replied a little grimly, and Hannah's eyes went misty with tears.

"I am so sorry, Grandma," she whispered, as they stepped out into the street.

"Never mind, lovey. Worse things happen at sea. Goodness, just look at the time. And it's snowing again. We'd best get a move on."

Hannah held tightly to Grandma's hand as they headed back to the station, a walk that seemed much longer then when they'd arrived. She felt wretched. Her feet hurt, her head hurt and worse than that was the ache of mortification in her chest.

"What carriage shall we take, Hannah, pet? Oh, I'm ready for a sit down. I'm fair exhausted."

"Number eight," she mumbled. It was the one she'd chosen that morning – eight because she was eight and a half and had thought herself grown up. Now she didn't feel grown up. Grown-ups didn't lose purses when they'd been trusted to buy something.

How could she tell Daddy? He called her his 'big girl,' but big girls who were trusted shouldn't lose things. Poor Grandma was out of pocket and so would Daddy be, because he'd have to pay Grandma back.

"There now, are you comfy?" Grandma gazed thoughtfully at Hannah. "You're tired, poppet. Cuddle close and have a sleep. Don't worry about that money. Your Daddy won't be cross. These things happen."

Hannah closed her eyes, for she knew that tears were going to squeeze from them again. She felt utterly miserable. She had let herself down and she'd let Daddy down. Was it because she had got 'too big for her boots'? She'd heard that expression recently. Now, to her shame, she knew what it meant.

Hannah snuggled close to Grandma, but the arm rest was in the way. She pushed it up, and as she did so, she heard a soft thud as something dropped on the cushion beside her. Through tear-filled eyes, she saw her lost purse lying on the worn moquette.

"Grandma! Look!" Hannah cried. "It must have got caught in the arm rest this morning."

"Is the money still there? Yes? Well, you are a lucky girl. Perhaps a Christmas angel was watching over you."

"Do you think so?" Hannah beamed. Then her face fell. "No, I was careless, Grandma, and I'm very sorry."

She handed over the three crisp ten shilling notes. "Thank you for paying for the stockings."

Grandma chuckled. "You're a funny one, Hannah Corkhill, but you're a lovely granddaughter, and if your new brother or sister is half as nice as you I'll be a very lucky lady."

Hannah flushed. No-one had ever paid her such a nice compliment.

As the train gathered speed, and Hannah stared out of the window into the snow flurried darkness, she thought over the happenings of the day. She'd been lucky all right, but she had been careless. Perhaps she wasn't quite as capable as Daddy thought.

The next thing Hannah knew, Grandma was shaking her gently awake. "I must get out now, Hannah. Only two stops to Ramsey, where Daddy will meet you. Thank you for being such good company. See you on Christmas Day."

Hannah kissed Grandma. The door banged and the train steamed out of Sulby station. Hannah sat up, smiling. Soon she would be home.

As the train neared the inkpot house, Hannah lowered the window. The incoming air was biting, though the snow had stopped and the sky was punctured with bright stars.

"It's nearly Christmas," Hannah whispered to herself, as the train began to slow and she gathered her things. "I feel I've been away for ages. I wonder how Mummy is?"

The train stopped and Hannah fumbled with the door, stepping out on to the dark platform apprehensively amidst the package laden shoppers.

"Hannah, Hannah!" Mick Corkhill came running towards her. "You've got a baby brother! What do you think of that?"

Hannah beamed. "Oh, Daddy, I'm so glad!" She threw her arms around him. "It's been such a long day and I've missed you."

"I've missed you too," Mick smiled. "Did you have a good time? Did you get the present for Mum?"

"Yes," Hannah nodded. She would admit her mishap later, but not now. Now all that mattered was to get home and see Mummy and the baby.

As she and her father ran from the station, Hannah realised that, though it was very nice to go shopping and have pennies to spend, there were some things that money could not buy. Some things were more precious than could be bought from any shop, even in Douglas.

48

Like a new baby.

No matter what might be in her Christmas stocking this year, nothing could be as exciting as a new baby brother!

GREEN HILLS OF HOME

Ballabeg

To be born here, to be at ease with, even to revel in the strictures of island life – as opposed to feeling stifled, as newcomers may – is a benefit we Manx rarely acknowledge until we go 'across,' and feel out of kilter. For many Manx folk the lure of home tugs like a piece of mental elastic, so that even as we marvel at a Niagara like cascade, or stare at a star studded desert sky a voice inside us says, 'There's near that much water in the 'fall at Glen Maye, an' I've seen better stars over Cronk y Voddey.' These reluctant travellers only truly relax when in sight of the island from the ferry, or when they finally step off the plane at Ronaldsway onto Manx soil, when their hearts give an uncontrollable leap of joy. This feeling, this indestructible link with the sights, sounds and smells of Mann is as perfect an explanation of 'sense of place' as I know.

This innate feeling, of belonging here and feeling at ease in all parts of the island, drives much of my writing. We Manx, the few amidst a mass nowadays, are remnants of indomitable generations. Tough country folk who struggled to live in harmony with the seasons and the land of their birth. God fearing, community minded and kindly, long may their like survive.

The chapel was full of homely souls in stout coats and mufflers. The calendar might denote that it was springtime but a sensible Manxman doesn't cast a clout till May's well out.

I slipped into my pew with my parents, aware of many eyes on me, though nowhere could I see the ones I was seeking.

I could hear murmurs as we settled. "He's lookin' poorly." And, "That's what city life does for a boy, though it's no more than he deserves, goin' off like that."

My mother's lips tightened. Her hearing had always been acute. I smiled inwardly, feeling oddly comforted by their whispering. Better being noticed than being ignored, I decided, and once they'd 'put a sight on me' a few times I knew my exploits 'across' would soon be old news.

The preacher arrived; Mr Jimson, a ruddy cheeked farmer and popular lay minister. A flurry of latecomers crept in and my heart gave a leap.

Jill had come after all.

"It'll be startin' soon." My mother nudged me. "Sit up, Daniel, you're slouchin'."

I sat up. No matter that I was going on twenty-six, and fresh from swinging London, in the days when it did swing. I knew that in my parents' eyes I would always be 'the young wun.'

I was staring at the back of Jill's head as we got up to sing the first hymn. She must have felt my gaze, for she turned and smiled and it was as though the dim wattage of the overhead bulbs had suddenly been turned up.

My mother elbowed me again. The singing had begun and I hadn't.

Cheerfully I joined in, swelling the formidable choruses. The tune was catchy, the words uncompromising, and every so often a phrase stood out, like a bright leaping herring in a stormy sea.

After the service as we shuffled towards the schoolroom my mother seemed more relaxed. "That'll have done you good, Daniel," she declared, her cheeks now pink, like mine felt.

Whether she was referring to the stirring sermon or the exercise for my still sluggish lungs I wasn't sure, Jill was still uppermost in my mind so I didn't pursue the matter. Would she and her mother stay for supper, or would she slip away now? I hoped not.

In a cheerful crush in the corridor, by some miracle, Jill and I were pushed within talking distance. I couldn't have planned it better.

"I wondered if you'd come, Daniel." She smiled. "Are you feeling better?"

"I am, thanks, but my, it's hot in here."

Jill grinned, and then we were swept apart. Mum was steering me before her into the schoolroom.

"Sit down, Daniel. The tea'll be along in a minute."

Hot tea was the last thing I needed. Frantically, I undid the buttons on my father's best tweed coat, which my mother had insisted I wear 'against the chill.'

"Now don't be catchin' cold," she exclaimed as I struggled out of the blanket heavy garment.

"Mum," I protested. She well knew I had myriad layers on beneath.

My father raised his eyebrows, cast me a knowing glance then swung his attention to the approaching trays and plates of food as though he'd long forgotten the high tea we'd sat down to only a couple of hours earlier.

"Have some sandwiches, lad." A well-filled plate was thrust beneath my chin. "You look as if you need feedin' up."

I took some, my eyes straining for a sight of Jill. I had hoped we would get a chance to talk. I knew I'd ruined any chance I ever had with her, but it would be nice to make my peace…

"Tea, Daniel?" a soft voice breathed in my ear. Jill stood before me, bearing a tray of brimming cups.

"Jillian, it's grand to see you," Mum cried. "It's Daniel's first outing since he got back. How do you think he's lookin'?

"Mother!" I said. "I'm not an exhibit."

Lifting two cups off the tray Mum tutted. "You looked a right exhibit when you got off that plane, collapsin' an' all." She pushed a cup and saucer into my hand and spooned in sugar unasked.

"He's a grown man – or so he says, Jillian. Yet he'd got himself in a proper state – in London." Mother almost spat the word. She had long regarded England's capital much as she regarded Sodom and Gomorrah.

Jill smiled as she moved away, and I gazed yearningly after her. She was even prettier than I remembered, no, she was beautiful now, there was a new maturity in her bearing that made me shrivel inside because of the way I'd treated her.

"Cake?" A plate piled with a variety of fruit, iced and fancy cakes was thrust under my nose. "Come on, Daniel, take a couple o'pieces. It's grand to see you back."

"Isn't it, Mr Jimson?" My mother beamed. "An' I'm hopin' he'll have the sense to stay here, on God's islan', instead of traipsin' again."

Meekly I helped myself to cake, while Dad heaped his plate. I munched obediently, until Mother turned away to speak to a couple at the next table and I decided that this was my chance. "I'll get a fill up of tea," I muttered, pushing my way through the chattering throng.

In the kitchen Jill was loading a tray with more cups.

"Can I help?" I asked and Jill's mother, Mrs Moore, beamed over the tea urn. "My word, Daniel, you're looking better. Do you really think you're up to helping though?

Jill looked at me doubtfully. "You can carry the sugar basin and some extra spoons, if you're determined."

"Of course!" I'd have set to and wiped the floor if she'd asked; anything to win back her approval. It was just a pity I'd not had as much sense two years earlier. If I had, Jill and I might have been enjoying our second year of marriage by now. Instead I had been unforgivably selfish. I'd thrown up my job and moved across impulsively, where I had proceeded to work myself practically into a nervous breakdown.

We'd already been engaged when I applied for the position I fancied in London, a top flight job with a matching salary. I hadn't told Jill until I was actually offered the post. I was as pleased as punch with myself and assumed she would be too.

She hadn't been, quite the opposite. "I can't believe you've done this without telling me, Daniel! You must have realised I wouldn't want to leave the island again just yet – if ever." She'd looked at me wonderingly, and something in her look made me realise how I'd grown to take her for granted.

"I spent three years at college, Daniel. "You knew how much I missed the place, and you, when I was away."

"So it's all right for you to get away but I can stay and stifle here when I could be forging a top class career across. I've worked hard too, you know. You're not the only one with qualifications. You just don't love me enough to move away with me, do you?"

I'd been selfishly blunt, as usual, yet even then Jill hadn't lost her temper. Looking back I cringe to think of that conversation. Jill had dealt with me as though I was one of her less intelligent pupils.

"It's not merely a matter of love, Daniel. Yes, I love you, but love isn't all that's needed in a relationship. There needs to be trust, and respect. Respect for ourselves as well as for each other. I know I'm needed here, and I'm staying. I'm sorry."

And she had stayed. We'd broken our engagement and I moved to London to my wonderful job, imagining I would soon be a wealthy man.

How naïve I was. Oh yes, London was all that I had imagined, and more, but work wasn't just a matter of doing my best for eight hours as it had been on the island. Work was pressure filled days of never less than ten hours, often twelve, sometimes longer. I barely had time to sleep before getting up again. That was when I could sleep.

Every day I commuted with more people than lived on the whole of the Isle of Man. I did make friends, some good friends too, and for almost eighteen months I deluded myself into imagining I was living life as it should be lived.

But one early Sunday morning as I slipped out for a pint of milk I heard a blackbird singing its heart out on a stunted tree stump on a street corner and I got an overwhelming gut-wrenching longing for home. I pictured myself walking up by Rushen Mines; staring at the view from the Sloc or striding up Bradda while seagulls wheeled overhead. I thought about the view from the Tower and the sensation of being buffeted by a good Manx gale, while scents of gorse and heather seared through my city clogged lungs.

I was an island man, but England was too big an island for me, and there was an empty place in my heart, which no one in London had filled. The memory of Jill's brown eyes began to slip into my mind often, too often, generally when I was in the midst of a meeting when I needed all my wits about me.

My boss was a considerate man; he suggested a break at home. Perhaps he could see what I could not – that though I was working to my utmost capacity; I was not succeeding, because I longed to be elsewhere…

"Sugar for Mrs Quillan, Daniel?" Jill nudged me gently. "Are you OK?"

"I'm fine," I said, and I was too. I'd known I'd be all right as soon as the plane came into land at Ronaldsway, and I glimpsed the familiar contours of coast, the landing strip and the countryside around. Gazing down at South Barrule and the snaking country road at the foot of it where my home lay, I'd felt a warm gladness surge through me.

Mind you, it didn't stop me making a fool of myself when I caught sight of my parents as I headed for the luggage carousel. I was suffering from a 'flu bug, as well as stress induced exhaustion, and after pulling my case off the revolving belt I passed out, onto a luggage trolley.

I was much stronger now and soon I would have an interview at the firm in Athol Street where I used to work.

"There, that's the lot," Jill took the sugar basin from me. "Would you like a fresh cup, Daniel, and some air? You're right, it is hot in here."

I followed Jill to the kitchen, and she poured tea into two cups from a homely brown teapot. We stood at the open back door and gazed into the darkness.

"Are you back for good, Daniel?"

I wondered what was coming. I knew she'd been seeing a local farmer... Mum had kept me abreast with all the gossip.

"I think so. I'm having an interview in Douglas Tuesday next. I reckon I've worked out my wanderlust."

"That's nice."

She took a hesitant breath, but I spoke before she had to.

"It's all right, Jill. I'm not presuming anything. How could I? Almost two years have passed and we're both different people. Well, I am anyway – I don't think you needed to change. I know I don't have a chance with you any more, and that's as it should be. But I would like to think we can still stay friends."

I drank my tea noisily in the silence that followed, while behind us the chatter and chink of teacups continued.

"I'd like us to be friends too, and I'm truly glad you've come back," Jill grinned at me with that impish grin that still made something quiver under my ribs.

"But you've not changed all that much Daniel Cannon. You still leap before you look. Have you realised what all the old gossips will be thinking, seeing you coming out here with me?"

"What? Oh Jill, I'm sorry. Honestly, I just wanted a chance to apologise. Let's go back in. I don't want to compromise your reputation."

In the Isle of Man, in the early Sixties, reputations still mattered.

Jill laughed. "Good," she said, and swung the outside door shut. "Now, you stand there, where everyone can see that we are not up to mischief and if you really want to prove to me that you're a changed man, you can dry these cups."

Before I realised what had happened I found myself with a drying cloth in my hand while Jill refilled the bowl with hot water.

"Oh, you can't let him do that," Mrs Moore cried, as she entered with a loaded tray. "And besides, his mum's looking for him."

"Tell her he's being useful," Jill said firmly. "I'm sure Mrs Cannon won't mind a few minutes more chat."

I grinned. Over the past few weeks I'd dreamed up every variation of meeting with Jill to apologise – mum, of course, had wanted me to ask her to tea - but that wouldn't have done at all.

If drying every cup, saucer and plate in the place would get me back in Jill's good books, then that was fine by me.

"There!" Jill said, when she'd almost done, and the capacious dresser was neatly stacked again. "That was a good team effort, wasn't it?"

"Daniel, your father's wantin' home. Are you goin' to be here all night?" My Mother, buttoning up her coat, saved me from replying.

"I'd better go," I said, holding out my damp tea towel.

Jill took it and laid it on the radiator. "Thank you Daniel, for your help."

"Any time," I said, avoiding her eyes.

"Oh, don't look so glum," Jill laughed as Mother fussed with my coat. "I'm glad I've seen you tonight, Dan. There's a Young Farmers' quiz on next week and I'm trying to raise a team. Are you interested? We could do with your brains."

If she was going to the quiz with her particular young farmer, I certainly wasn't interested. I would hate it.

"It's for charity," she said persuasively, and my mother prodded me in the back. She'd been telling me it was time I got out and about again.

"If Mum can spare me, I'm your man." I put my arm round Mum and gave her a hug.

"Oh, you," Mother protested but I could see she was pleased. She flicked little glances around the emptying hall as if to say – 'Look now, he's not too grown up to appreciate his old mother.'

Well, she was right. I did appreciate her and Dad, and all they'd done for me. Not that I totally regretted moving away. It had helped me grow up, and made me realise what was important in life, and more precious than any highly paid job.

Through my heedless behaviour I had thrown up a wonderful relationship, and I had hurt Jill, which was unforgivable. I would have to earn her respect, if ever we were to be true friends again. .

"Say goodnight to Jillian, Daniel," Mother ordered, as though I was a child still.

But I wasn't a child, and neither was Jill. As she took my hand

and I felt the warmth of her fingers and as our eyes met I felt a surging relief. The past did stand for something after all, and I knew that despite everything, we were still friends.

That was all I needed. The future was an uncharted path. If I trod carefully, perhaps one day Jill's steps and mine might converge.

IT CAN'T BE EASY TO BE DEAD

Cronk ny Arrey Laa

This story might seem odd. It is odd, I suppose, but it is based on reality and experience. Not mine, necessarily.

One has to leave one's remains somewhere, and scattered atop the grandeur of Cronk ny Arrey Laa seems ideal for a final 'fling.' Better than having a burial and leaving one's descendants, should one have any, obligated to look after one's plot for ever.

We are all but leaves that blow off the tree of life with dispiriting regularity - or uplifting frequency - should you have sufficient faith as to be truly certain that 'the best is yet to come.'

I have faith, I don't have certainty, but I can appreciate the glory that is beyond understanding, and death, like life, is undeniably enigmatic. The grim reality of its aftermath occasionally deserves a brisk no nonsense approach.

I wondered, as I struggled up the hill, bent on scattering Gerald's ashes, whether they wouldn't have been more usefully scattered on my compost heap. It was perhaps a heartless reflection, but being bereaved doesn't remove one's propensity for heartlessness. Besides, I was feeling nauseous, and nausea always makes me snappy. The hill was steep, steeper than I remembered, and for sure, Gerald wouldn't have got this far.

What would he have done, if he'd been in my place? Get a taxi driver to nip up here? Yes, I can imagine him doing exactly that. We've no neighbours who are fit enough, and as for family, well...

Our romantic decision regarding what the remaining one of us would do when the other popped their clogs now seemed ludicrous. We'd made our wills fifteen – no seventeen - years ago when we were both a great deal more active. Certainly Gerald, reduced as he was to the urn full of ashes I was carrying could hardly be less active.

We should have foreseen the eventuality of old age, but who does?

Who, if they're honest, ever envisages the years of infirmity before they arrive? Certainly we hadn't, and to be brutally honest I knew we'd both been sliding downhill, mentally and physically for years.

"Buck up, woman," I told myself. "This won't do."

I wasn't often given to maudlin speculation, especially whilst being buffeted by a fearsome gale on a remote hilltop, with my feet planted in a scatter of rabbit droppings, but I'd had to pause, to catch my breath, and the utter ridiculousness of this venture suddenly occurred to me. I wondered had it crossed Gerald's kindly but decidedly woolly mind in his last days?

Our joint wills stipulated that whoever went first should scatter the other on this particular hill. If we both went at the same time the task was left to our executors. If only we had, it would have made things a lot less exerting.

And to ask a taxi driver to fulfil the obligation would hardly have been playing the game, would it?

Gerald had been mobile, in a limited, bungalow sort of manner until the end; in fact the day before he died he tripped me up at least twice with his dratted stick. Should our positions have been reversed I daresay the old buzzard, as I'd fondly called him for years, might have squeezed through the narrow kissing gate I'd just manoeuvred myself through, some moments before, but not without difficulty.

Then? Yes, I could imagine the ensuing scenario. He would have taken one look at the steep path leading uphill and would have tipped me out, not giving a toss about all the mud filled ruts just inside the gate, which is where I'd have landed.

I'd have been trampled by every walker for months till quite absorbed into the landscape.

"Well, I've done you better than that, my darling buzzard," I declared, tucking my gloves into my pocket, the better to tackle opening the urn, for I had recovered my breath sufficiently to do the deed.

As I unscrewed the lid I gazed at the panoramic view, smugly pleased that I'd reached my goal so speedily. It was barely eleven o'clock and here I was, already at the teeth-chattering top. Despite my thermals, boots and hat and mighty exertion, I was perished.

I will be honest here. I had been greatly tempted not to come. When I'd opened the curtains that morning and spotted a skim of frost on the birdbath it crossed my mind that if I scattered Gerald in the garden along with the bird-bread no one would be any the wiser.

Compost heap or roses, he could have benefited both and I wouldn't have had to step out of my cosy slippers and dressing gown. If I'd taken that easy way out I'd be snug at home now making a cup of chocolate for my elevenses, instead of listening to my false teeth chatter.

"Still, here I am, so I might as well get it done."

With some difficulty I prised open the lid and swung the container in a wide arc. A gust of wind promptly blew the contents into my face making me cough, and laugh.

"Oh Gerald, what a hoot!" My shout was loud but my words were utterly lost against the wind. I turned, and emptied out the remainder..

The brittle grains lay scattered upon the scorched heather like over-enthusiastic seasoning. I could hardly believe the meagre amount I'd tipped from the cask was really all that remained of Gerald and his fine mahogany coffin. I suppose one must trust the crematorium staff, a lucrative sideline on recycled coffins is not the sort of entrepreneurship a grieving person likes to dwell upon.

I upended the container one final time – my, it was an ugly little thing, and the last grains drifted away. I felt a horrid pang. Not that I hadn't experienced several such since Gerald's passing, but this was a particularly resonant pang. It shifted my insides and a slight nausea recurred.

The funeral tasks were all complete. Now I had to face my solitary future. It was a daunting prospect, and standing on that bare hilltop with the wind pulling at my woollen hat and my legs still trembling from the climb it was not one that I viewed with any relish. I gazed at the bright winter sky with its sharp edged clouds and tried to summon brisk, positive thoughts, though truly I felt rather gloomy. I daresay a relieving weep might have done me good, but crying is such a messy business and I needed to shop on my way home. The funeral mourners had eaten me out of bread, cheese, and gin. Besides, it wasn't exactly sadness that was dragging me down; it was more a nagging irritation.

Gerald was dead and gone. I'd scattered his remains, I'd cleared out his clothes. I'd even chucked out his pipes, though I'd kept his knobbly walking stick. It might come in useful soon enough. Yet the old buzzard was still communicating with me; talking, badgering in fact, and I wished he'd shut up.

It wasn't an unnerving occurrence. I'm not the nervous kind and Gerald never said boo to an avoidable goose when he was alive. No, it was as though Gerald could not, or would not let me go, which was a pity; because I wished he'd put a sock in it and shine stars or be an angel or whatever it is that the dead customarily do. When alive he'd long been indecisive. It seemed now that he was dead he was still in a quandary.

Gerald's latest interjection, only moments before, had been to contradict me over my use of the word *mountain*. In all our years together Gerald had never been able to read my thoughts. Half the time he had barely been able to read my lips. He'd been deaf for years. Now he could read my mind. That wasn't fair. 'Not cricket,'as Gerald himself would have been the first to point out.

"Yes, I am well aware that Cronk ny Arrey Laa is not a mountain, as it's not high enough, but I do wish you wouldn't keep doing this, Gerald. You're dead." I swung round. "Do you know I can almost smell your stinking old pipe?"

Having a tissue to hand I blew my nose noisily, thus quelling Gerald's caustic rejoinder. "That will do," I said firmly, wiping my nose and determinedly surveying the scene, which was magnificent.

The hill, yes note I am using the word *hill* of Cronk ny Arrey Laa, or *Hill of the Day-Watch*, which is the meaning of the name in Manx Gaelic, is dramatically situated, its summit rising above high moorland while its western flank sweeps precipitately down to rocks and the crashing Irish Sea. Across a quarter mile stretch of sheep grazed land to my left was the greater height of South Barrule, which, though again not a mountain, was a challenging rise, crowned by a fascinating Iron Age hill fort, a more strenuous climb than this, and one I doubt I will make again. Beyond Barrule I could see the extending undulating spinal range, the backbone of the Isle of Man, stretching to the north and Snaefell, our one and only Manx mountain.

I waited for an interjection, but none came. I was able to resume my meditation.

It does one so much good to get up onto the hills. To look down upon the lowlands, in which so much of our petty lives are set, puts life, and indeed death, in a more understandable perspective. In fact climbing to the hilltops on a regular basis is in my opinion, essential to retain one's sanity. Do you know there are young people born and bred on the island who have never climbed a Manx hill! It makes me furious, this deliberate turning away from the land.

The land of our birth shapes us. Well, it has shaped me, certainly, and Gerald was always an outdoors man, bless him. We met in a walking group I joined when I returned to the island after having lived for more than thirty years on that frenetic 'other isle.' The group were mostly old fogies, but Gerald immediately struck me as being different from the usual 'when I' types who retire over here. I seem to recall we enjoyed a tremendous argument on our first outing. He said the Manx were a backward looking race. I disagreed vehemently. It was an auspicious beginning. A good argument is so exhilarating. Gerald was nothing like my first husband, thank God, though what he thought of me initially I dread to ponder. Whacky, possibly? Batty more likely. Especially as I'm afraid I did rather throw myself at him. Sometimes I wondered at my behaviour, but I have no time for women who say they don't need a man. Besides, when we met Gerald still possessed a rugged allure, which I found excessively arousing. I wished I'd met him twenty years earlier. I'd have chucked my husband without a qualm in his favour. When it became apparent, after only a few weeks of acquaintance that Gerald felt as I did and that he was prepared to worship the ground I trampled upon, I moved out of my poky Douglas flat and into his rather nice bungalow in Colby. We married a year later.

This particular location, near the summit cairn, was our favourite picnic spot. We'd come here half a dozen times each season when we were first married, though I confess we haven't been here for two or more years now. Anno Domini, how it does impede one's physical desires. Talking of physical desires – no I shan't. Some things are better left un-described. Suffice to admit that we were well over pensionable age when we celebrated our anniversary in a particularly physical manner up here one memorable summer's day. Gerald was into his seventies then, but still extremely able.

I chuckled. Now that memory did make me feel better. It warmed me almost as much as the flask of hot tea waiting in my car.

I patted a nearby clump of heather, thereby dislodging the granular remains of Gerald. "Goodbye, for now, my love," I whispered as I pulled on my gloves. It was another moment when tears were near, but the wind was bitter and I hadn't time to weep.

"Besides, it would be different if I wasn't going to hear from you again," I said hopefully.

"That's right," Gerald agreed. Good gracious, he'd never replied so promptly when he was alive!

"Hmph!" I tutted. "I hope you aren't going to be with me forever."

There was no reply this time, but a rather cold silence.

"I suppose you think me callous," I remarked, as I slithered down the steepest part of the pathway – risking a broken ankle several times and reflecting that if I did tumble I might lie undiscovered for quite some time. I have not succumbed to purchasing one of those annoying mobile phones and I have no intention of doing so. Modern technology can go hang, as far as I am concerned. I dislike being contacted unexpectedly. I even frequently unplug the phone at home when I don't want to talk.

This desire for peace was another reason why I objected to Gerald still being in touch. I couldn't unplug a supernatural contact could I? I'd have to put up with him, unless he got side tracked into bothering someone else.

"For goodness' sake, there must be enough interesting folk up there to chat to?"

Another silence. Perhaps at last he'd taken the hint.

I don't think I'm ready for heaven. Think of meeting all your old friends and family in one huge emotional confrontation. Good Lord. That's not heaven. That's the other place.

"You shouldn't make light of such things," Gerald declared, in the portentous way he'd had when he really wanted to get on my nerves.

"Shut up, Gerald," I said tartly. "I've done my bit for you today. You can close down now. I want to enjoy the rest of my walk."

"I'm not a machine," Gerald said. "You seem to be treating me as though I can do something about this. I'm as troubled by it as you. It's not what they led me to believe."

"What? What? Oh, you'll have to be quiet; there are two walkers coming towards me. I can't have them seeing me talking to myself."

"You don't need to talk, though, do you, darling? You can just think your reply to me."

I glowered, but altered my expression hurriedly. "Good morning," I said brightly to the young couple in passing. They were dressed in drab army colours and had woollen hats pulled down over

65

their ears like bank robbers. Does anyone look in a mirror nowadays? I like to look well turned out whatever the situation. "Isn't it a lovely day for a walk?" I smiled. They mumbled something and strode on.

"You always knew how to dress," Gerald said in my ear, and then added softly, "and undress..."

"Gerald," I yelped aloud, then turned and waved gaily to the receding young couple who'd looked back at my cry.

I pointed to my ankle and pretended to limp. They looked at one another and I hoped they wouldn't come to my aid. I waved again and stumbled on. "Drat," my ankle was actually hurting.

Within a few moments I reached the kissing gate. I pressed the bar but it refused to open. I pushed it harder.

"Sorry," Gerald whispered. His voice was very faint now. I could barely hear him.

"Never mind sorry," I snapped. "I want to get back to the car. I'm frozen to the marrow." I gave the bar another tentative push and the gate flew open.

"Oh Gerald," I sighed. "I didn't mean to snap. I'm sorry too, I'm very sorry that you've gone."

The metal of the road rang under my boots. It was a brisk hundred-yard walk to my car, tucked into a gateway. I unlocked the door, plumped into the seat and reached for the thermos of tea.

"Ahh!" My breath steamed the windscreen as I drank. From my comfortable seat I could still make out the cairn at the summit. It was good to know that Gerald would always have that grandeur about him; that wide expanse of sky, the sheer drop to the sea one side, the southern plain and all our homely familiar haunts on the other.

"I'll miss you, Gerald, darling," I said, "and if you must keep talking to me I don't mind. Really I don't. It can't be easy to be dead."

I waited, and listened, but no response echoed in my mind.

"How curious," I remarked, and after a few moments, as my feet were getting chilly, I started the engine and drove away.

I glanced back at the hill once more, before my descent into the valley.

A bird was hovering over the summit, a brown and white bird of prey, balancing, with ponderously beating wings, on the wind.

"A buzzard!" Well, goodness me. No wonder Gerald had stopped talking to me. The dear man had been transformed into what I'd always suspected was his destiny.

As I drove towards home I felt alternately elated and downcast.

"Take care, Gerald," I murmured parking outside the Spar shop at Colby and reaching for my shopping bag. "I daresay I'll be with you soon."

LANDFALL II

Maughold

I find the ruined keeills of the Island fascinating, situated as many are in the loneliest regions, yet often with the grandest of outlooks; their occupiers must have been men of exemplary mental and physical powers. Merely contending with the elements and keeping body and soul together would be hardship enough, but many of these hermits, lay brothers, Culdees, call them what you will, were skilled builders, herbalists and foragers as well as being healers and learned holy men, who helped others as well as living lives of prayer and contemplation.

In my first book of short stories, Climbing to Cregneash, I introduced Alan, a diffident, awkward, lay brother, washed up on the shores of Mann after surviving a terrifying voyage in a flimsy coracle. He had fled the dour regime of a northern Abbey where indifference and cruelty was the norm, rather than God's loving kindness.

From the moment he was spewed ignominiously onto the rocky coast of Mann Alan vowed that he would devote his life to God in thanks for his miraculous deliverance. This resolution was ambitious, considering his formerly erratic relationship with the Supreme Being.

Despite overwhelming odds, his feeble faith included, Alan achieves some of what he intended. Another winter has passed. It is a watery spring day...

Alan was unwell. This was not an uncommon condition – he'd coped with loose bowels and an unhappy digestion many times since he'd been tossed like a piece of seaborne wrack upon the shores of Mann. This malaise was different, however, a raging fever had taken hold of him with such severity he had no option but to succumb and take to his bed. As the Sabbath dawned he found he could not raise his head from his bracken pillow, and the effort incurred in trying to, made his pulse race almost as fast as when he climbed Barrule. Although it was the day he regularly offered Mass to his small flock he knew, by the pounding of his head and the drumming of his heart that this day he must let them, and God, down.

This realisation was awful. Alan trembled uncontrollably, his head and limbs afire, his muddled thoughts precluding anything practical, save a mumbled prayer that time and God's grace might bring healing. This effort made his head ache more, lucidity waned and Alan's cluttered mind became burdened by the darkest of images. His imaginings became fearful. Maybe he was en route to the deepest sleep of all, and if so, should he try do fight this state, or give in? Was he not heart weary from battling this never-easy state of mortality? Why not endure the final judgement and submit, without delay, to Purgatory?

"I have t-tried my best," he babbled. "What m-man could do more? G-god will surely understand my f-failings and f-forgive?"

Had Alan been in his right mind he would have felt considerable apprehension about facing up to his maker's final judgement. He was still far from the threescore years and ten he had hoped to wrest from life, and his desire to make some worthy contribution, no matter how small, in this vale of tears, was still hopelessly unfulfilled.

"D-does God even c-care?" He muttered pitifully. "What is the p- point of struggling? It will be s-simpler to g-give in and g-give up.

Easier, much easier..." As Alan tossed, dozed and dreamed fiery, terrible dreams he had not the wit, the energy or, for once, the conscience, to quest or heed. In a burning torpor he slumped, too feeble, after some hours, even to moan.

Dawn trumpeted its arrival with a cacophony of birdsong and merry fingers of sunshine poking through the rough-hewn gap high in the east wall of his hand built dwelling. Alan turned his face to the sun and hoped its warming rays might have healing in their benison. As the hours passed, the cheerful birdsong died, clouds gathered above his little shelter and soon a customary gloom fell on the piled sod and stone walls and flimsy strutted eaves of beech and ash, cut from a nearby copse and fashioned more by luck than by skill. The resulting roof with its meagre thatch was waterproof in only the lightest shower, for it had many gaps. Indeed the entire construction gave little protection from the elements, yet its existence, in the early days, had imbued Alan with joy and justifiable pride. For the first time in his life he had a place to call his own, in which to live work and pray.

Since arriving on the shores of Mann Alan had rarely been idle. Even before his shelter was complete he sought out the scattered tribes and families of his region, talking with them and praying for them. He asked nothing in return. His method of conversion was to suggest, rather than exhort, he was content that his neighbours knew he was near. He hoped that he had by now earned their acceptance, if not their trust.

The simplicity of his existence had adequately sustained Alan's mind, as had plants and natural food sources sustained his body. Before arriving on Mann Alan's life had been a dismal rote of hardship and disappointments. His new life initially infused him with hope, for each day and the future. Though his habits were still of necessity the simplest and most Spartan, Alan dealt eagerly with each day's possibilities, always welcoming change and new challenges.

Until now; at a stroke this severe malaise had robbed him of faith and optimism, indeed as the ague shivers increased he felt all positivity gushing from him, like a mud slide in a flood, leaving his mind an abandoned husk. A weighty blanket of pessimism oppressed him, extinguishing all but dread thoughts. He lay, panting, exhausted,

70

terrified, sure his end must soon come, and God speed it, for this torment was the worst he had known.

His nostrils twitched. The scent of good roast meat teased his senses. Surely the devils of hell were not heating their fires already? Did burning flesh smell like this? His dryness of mouth increased as his salivary glands tried vainly to soothe his rasp dry throat. He stirred anxiously. The smell was intoxicating. Surely his fevered imagination had undergone this torture earlier, when vivid images of fat roast fowls and scrumptious pies, such as had been served on feast days at the Abbey had floated through his dreams? Not that Alan had ever tasted such delicacies, or even glimpsed them on the white clothed tables of the refectory, relegated as he had been to the foulest kitchen duties, but he had seen the returned plates and smelled the leavings, delicious morsels of such succulence that Alan had once accused the cook, a filthy wretch otherwise, of possessing angelic talents. This compliment had earned him a wallop with a basting spoon and a kick in the direction of the overflowing voider basket.

He whimpered in his dreams. This memory still pained him. Carrying the basket of leftovers to the Abbey gates had been one of Alan's regular duties. His natural compassion would have been assuaged had the voider basket been heaped with choice leavings. It was not; all that was good had already been filched by the castle underlings and the basket was regularly crammed with rotten vegetables and mouldy scraps, fit only for pigs or rats.

Yet the rabble of humanity who waited with such eagerness, at the stipulated distance from the Abbey gates, most no more than scrag and bone themselves, pounced upon the food as though it was manna, rifling the basket with such vicious ferocity that as Alan clung to the cold stone gate post he sometimes feared they might next tear the flesh from his bones in their hunger.. When the basket was at last empty the beneficiaries, even the ragged urchins, still had energy to curse him, as if it was his fault that the leavings had not been better or more plentiful.

In his fever Alan groaned; such memories rankled, like raw wounds, constantly chafed by the sad fact that men refused to care for one another as Christ dictated. Why? Why did mankind not wish to share God's loving kindness and the good earth's abundance willingly? Why did daily life never get near to the life promised by God?

A chink, as of wood on iron startled Alan. In his fevered state images of ravening beasts, red eyed, with slavering jaws, intent on tearing him limb from limb, provoked unmanly tears to roll down his fevered cheeks. The scent of meat grew stronger. Was he entering the halls of Hell already? Had he by-passed judgement and purgatory – was he not considered fit enough even for that?

A stealthy whisper, a shadowed nearness, a touch on his cheek, sent shivers of near licentious pleasure through him. A mountain stream, a distillation of exquisite sweetness fell moistly upon his caked eyelids, clearing his sight to unimagined brightness. So startling was this that a wriggling shoot of hope stirred within him, feebly frail, yet resilient, like a bud in spring.

He tried, vainly, to raise his head.

"Hush brother, lie still."

It was a woman's voice, a dulcet voice, brimming with human charity, provoking further tears to gush down his cheeks.

A laugh, low now, another voice, less fine, but also kind, confused his senses as a resinous, herb scented balm was smoothed upon his brow by delicate fingers.

"Angels?" He tried to sign the cross on his chest, but his fingers would not move. "H-have pity," he croaked, "I h-have nothing to r-reward you but f-fever."

A fist appeared before his tortured eyes. Alan awaited a blow but the arm burrowed under his pillow to raise his head.

"Drink, thee, brother. I'm no angel." Alan smelled rank human breath and relaxed.

Warm meat juice coursed down his throat, making him retch.

"Easy now, brother, Easy."

His swimming eyes could make out nothing but the lip of a wood cup and a tangle of hair. The broth was shockingly reviving; as he drank he felt his strength surge like an incoming tide.

"Thou will do." The voice said as his head was returned to his pillow. "Sleep more, brother. Rest. We'll come again."

A shaft of light crossed Alan's face as the visitors left, passing the woven hurdle back across his doorway. In his bemused state, he was surprised that Angels needed to exit through the door. It was comforting, though, knowing that angels were near. That knowledge and the good meat broth made Alan's subsequent sleep of a deeper, healing kind.

Twice more he was disturbed from his dreams by angelic presences, and twice more he felt the cooling streams upon his forehead and tasted the rich broth that to his troubled mind had hints of ambrosia within its alluring depths.

Still he was content to accept, not question and as the sun rose and the moon died Alan slept, long and hard.

When next he woke it was nightfall, and this time it was rain pattering on his face and pillow that awakened him. Alan blinked into the darkness, and knew himself to be, if not healed, then come once more to his senses. There was a dismal satisfaction in this, mixed with regret. It would have been good to be taken to heaven, or whatever waiting room of heaven in which the likes of he would be accommodated. He would have been grateful for the least important side room. Instead he had still to cope, not only with the rigours of life but the fact that God seemed always to be out of spirit with him. He must surely know that the past days had been difficult, and yet…

"I'll r-really t-try to p-please you, God," he murmured, "if only you will s-stop the r-rain c-coming through my roof."

As if in reply, the rain fell heavier. Alan had to force himself off his couch and with weak, shaky limbs and bleary concentration pull his bed closer to the eaves, where the drips disturbed less.

"The r-roof must be m-made g-good before w-winter – should I live so l-long," Alan sighed, acknowledging that now the bleak reality of existence stretched before him once more, he felt curiously saddened. He must take up the burden of life again. Not yet though, he was still weak and weary.

Alan dozed for several hours, until once more dawn lightened his window. This time when he woke the old urge of conscience pricked him. The least he could do, as he had come through the valley of death was to celebrate Mass. He must rise, at whatever cost and put this worthy intention into practice.

Alan lay unmoving, contemplating the difficulties involved in this simple act. Then he closed his eyes, for a quiet inner voice reminded him that should he move too soon his recovery might be slowed, not hastened. He determined to lie on, but nevertheless felt again the prickle of guilt which his illness had, for a short time, removed. He stirred, groaned and stretched a shaky leg towards the floor.

"Thee better then?" Some hours later, this question, rudely put, and accompanied by a putrescent stench of fish as a figure entered unannounced, disturbed Alan, on his knees in prayer.

"I saw the smoke of your fire from beyond the hill. You feel better, then?"

Alan nodded shakily, his rosary slipping from his fingers. Who was this grubby apparition? Clothed in skins and rags, the man, or was it woman, leered, as if she knew him well. That could not be. No woman knew him, in any sense of the word.

"Thee will need to get roused. A swarm of new settlers've come ashore in a pitiful state. Shipwrecked, after a bloody sea battle, they say. They've been questing for you."

Grim fantasies of the Abbey brothers vengefully travelling across the sea to do him harm made Alan almost swoon. He trembled and what residue of spirit he'd regained shrank with dread. If only he had died while in the grip of the debilitating fever. By now he could have left this vale of tears and been with the Lord. "Q-questing for me? Why? I h-have n-nothing, I am n-nothing."

The creature - woman-kind he now suspected, from the thrusting mounds above her plaited belt, rubbed her palms almost with glee.

"They're believers, brother; they want your blessing to help 'em against we heathens!" She yelped delightedly and aimed a playful punch at Alan's middle.

Alan winced, his ribs contracting, reawakening his retching cough.

"Sit now, brother, save your breath," the woman said, though not unkindly, pushing him onto his bed, fondling his scruffy hair as though patting a favoured dog. There's bread here, and a hunk of new cheese." She gestured to a bundle tied in a cloth on his altar stone. "Eat it soon. It won't last." She surveyed him ruefully. "You're nobbut gristle and bone, you need feeding up. Get these settlers to forage for you. You help them, they will fend for you, do you see?"

Allan's eyes brimmed. "You've b-brought me f-food again? Why such k-kindness?"

"Why not? Should we have let you die when you were rambling with fever?"

Allan felt humbled. "I d-don't know you y-yet you o-offer nourishment and h-help. Do you t-take Mass?"

"My man does. I've no hankering for redemption or life after death. Preaching plucks no fowls."

Alan was taken aback by her reply. Yet he could not but respect her.

She turned to go as he unwrapped the course cloth and found a quartern loaf and a hunk of soft sweet cheese. His mouth watered. "M-may G-god bless and k-keep you," he murmured tearfully.

"Aye," the woman grunted. "And you. Now don't be forgetting what I said. Get them shipwrecked sinners organised. They'll think better of you if you show them leadership."

"I w-will," Alan scrambled to his feet. "Shall I g-go now?"

She laid a sturdy hand on his shoulder. "Stay, I'll get my man to direct them here. Sit and eat, brother. Restore yourself." She tightened her fingers. "They'll not respect you, else."

Alan nodded, impressed by her firmness and her evident strength.

The woman flashed him a gap toothed smile and left, banging the door hurdle.

Alan nibbled at the cheese and bread, sipped water and wished his insides did not feel so weak and his heart so irresolute. Yet another challenge had been sent to test him, a challenge he was in no shape to meet. Yet he had no choice.

The cheese and bread were succulent but substantial enough for him to stomach only a little. He wrapped the remains and pushed them onto the window shelf. The sight of the two bundles suddenly swept him back to the Abbey and a pantry which had been full of similar homely packages, propitiate offerings from sinners rich and poor eager to gain indulgences; a custom as confusing as simony to Alan. Was God really in favour of such practices?

The moment was not opportune to dwell on theological matters. He had time only to splash his face with water and smooth his rough thatch of hair before he heard a murmur of distant voices. His new flock were approaching.

Tying his girdle tight around his shrunken waist and adjusting his rosary, Alan picked up his staff and stepped through the doorway on still shaky legs.

The sight that met his eyes shocked and initially daunted him. Only his legs were so feeble he might have retreated. A vast collection of souls was advancing from the direction of the bay, men, women and children.

Alan took half a dozen steps towards them and stood, trembling, his heart's loud beating gradually shutting out all sounds of nature and the murmurings from the folk as they neared.

He breathed gustily, expelling by exhalation, his fears, urging his painfully beating heart to slow, his face to assume a welcoming expression, for God alone must have directed these people to him, and with a purpose. He must be steadfast for God's and his own sake.

As his heart slowly calmed a brief recount of the multitude reassured him. The vast collection was actually no more than forty. Ragged, wretched, pitiful wrecks of beings, with raddled features and strained, fearful expressions, most barely skin and bone, some with recent wounds and blood stained rags around their limbs, even the children looked like the saddest of souls.

Alan's thoughts swept back to his own unannounced arrival on this blessed isle. To cross the ocean unharmed had been an epiphany in itself. To endure the terror of shipwreck and worse – what had his succouring nurse told him about these folk? That they'd been caught in 'A bloody sea battle.' What fearful experiences must they have endured, what grim experiences - and with women and infants to protect, how much greater their travail than any he had known?

Alan's trembling hands lifted, in a gesture of welcome. To his delight he found his beating heart calm, his lips began, of their own inclination, to utter the mid-day prayer, which was right for the moment, he knew, by the cast of the sun and the feel of the wind on his body. He fingered his rosary, closed his eyes and gave his spirit to God.

76

The approaching flock paused some yards away, their faces wary, fathers pushing their children behind them, mothers clutching babies to their breasts.

Alan finished his prayer and smiling, walked towards them, his arms wide.

"W-welcome, brothers, s-sisters and l-little ones. God has protected and g-guided you to my humble d-door. Rest here and I will fetch w-water and f-food." He turned, but one of the foremost, a black eyed slattern, with eager face, accompanying a man with a bloody arm limped towards him.

"Nay, Master, show me, and I will serve you. You are needed amongst us, we have undergone dreadful happenings," her lip trembled. "We need your comfort and your prayers."

Alan laid his hand on the woman's head and felt a shudder of resolve pass through him. These poor bereft souls, his heart went out to them. He must succour them as much as he was able, with God's help.

A murmur ran through the watching crowd as he made the sign of the cross over her dark hair. The woman smiled, looking up at him trustingly. The tension of the crowd lessened, mothers set down their babies, and men helped their older fellows to the ground. "Thank you, s-sister. You will find b-bread and cheese on the w-window shelf. There is w-water aplenty in the b-brook over y-yonder. And there are herbs a-and cress a-plenty on its b-banks."

The woman nodded. "A j-jug and c-cup stands with the f-food," he added kindly as a ragged waif moved from the encircling arm of the injured man. "Yes, your h- help is w-welcome too, child, take my hand, I w-will show you where we m-may pick b-berries."

The child held out his small hand and Alan grasped it, feeling the warm heat of it with a leap of joy and a transforming sense of calm. He knew not from where this inner calm had come, nor how his feelings of ill health had so swiftly fled. He was aware only of peace and certainty rising within him, a sensation that all he had been and all that he had undergone had prepared him for this day.

He moved amongst the people, talking quietly, his face lit by the deep well of compassion which had always lived in his heart, though long hidden by his lack of self-belief.

The bread was broken, the cheese divided, berries and herbs were shared, and sweet water from the brook. Almost as in the gospel of the loaves and fishes, there were crumbs for all.

Alan sat, his arms around two smiling infants, naught but skin and bone, yet cheerful, as was he, aware that this was what God had prepared him for, to care for these unhappy souls and to teach them the joys of the true Christian faith.

Alan had never known the love of family. Now, with two small bodies nestling against him and with the trust of so many eyes upon him he realised what he had missed. A disconcerting serenity suffused him and he wondered whether he was worthy of such joy.

As the birdsong in the nearby trees quietened and the shadows lengthened over the slopes of Barrule Alan gently moved away the now sleeping infants and stood to celebrate Mass, not inside his tiny cell, but in the open air, God's own church.

The rich Latin words were as comforting as nourishment to the stricken people, and as Alan blessed his small flock at the final Amen he felt that at last, that day, he might - possibly - have earned God's approval.

LOVE ME DO

Douglas

The nineteen sixties were for me a decade of change. In May 1960 my mother died suddenly, I was twelve. By the age of fifteen and a half I had finished a secretarial course and in the summer I helped at a B & B at St John's. I then worked a few months as a receptionist before moving to a position as office junior in the General Office of Dowty Engineering, at Castle Hill, Douglas, within easy walking distance of "Woodville" my home in Victoria Road.

In the mid-1960s Dowty's changed their name to Iloman Engineering and moved to a new factory in School Road, Onchan. I travelled by bus each day to the works, to type letters and invoices, operate an accounting machine, assist with the weekly cash pay-out and ultimately to monitor monthly sales figures. In August 1965 I became engaged, I was married in April 1967. In the spring of 1968 I left Dowty's on maternity leave.

By the end of the decade I was preparing to move from our second marital home, a police house, into Onchan Police Station, with my police constable husband and baby daughter. Ten years of considerable change. Ten years in which the Beatles provided the backing tracks to my life.

Hilary gazed at the receding Steam Packet vessel, Manx Maid, her vision blurred by tears and too much mascara. This morning she'd put loads on - too much Mum had said over breakfast - when Leo was packing. But she'd wanted to look good for him, on this, his last morning.

She gave a final wave, though she could barely make out his tiny figure on the top deck of the vessel by now. "Goodbye, Leo," she quavered, dabbing her eyes and tucking her windblown hair behind her ears. Doing this reminded her of Leo and his first words to her. She began to run, trying to rid herself of the heartache that was welling inside her.

"You look like Sandie Shaw." Leo had said, that first day, cheekily flicking her auburn bob. Sitting next to him on a horse tram Hilary pretended to be offended. She tried to give him a chilling glance, but she couldn't. She'd smiled and dimpled, feeling flattered to think she resembled the famous bare foot singer. Hilary adored pop music and followed the starry exploits of all the big names in the New Musical Express, their fantastic Carnaby-Street lives seeming a world away from the not so 'swinging' Isle of Man.

Few pop stars visited Douglas, even though the Mersey was only a boat trip away. Neither the Beatles nor Cilla Black, or even Gerry and the Pacemakers had thought to step on an Isle of Man ferry to visit their Manx fans. Maybe one day, Hilary hoped. For now she would continue to dream about them and collect their singles. Whereas Leo had seen them all, in the flesh!

Hilary ran even faster, much too fast for her not very sensible but ever so 'with it' purple strappy shoes bought just before Leo's visit from Saxone. She knew she should slow down but she just couldn't.

She had to shift some of the awful wrenching ache beneath her ribs that had started that morning because of having to say goodbye to Leo.

"How will I live without him?" She wailed into the biting wind, a wind so chill it stung her cheeks and made her mascara laden eyes water even more.

Hilary had spent months looking forward to the past weekend, yet it had fled in an instant and now the rest of her life stretched bleakly, Leo-less, before her. They had been writing and telephoning each other for months, full of excitement as to what they'd do and where they'd go when they met. It was last July when they'd first met on that fateful horse tram, clopping along Douglas Prom. A lad Leo had come on holiday with had abandoned him to go off with a girl and Leo had been on his own, trying to make the best of things in a strange place. Hilary hadn't minded his picking her up. She'd been fed up because her girl-friend had let her down and she was on her own that day too, so meeting Leo had been lucky. He'd been polite yet funny and she'd been attracted and amused by his cheeky Liverpool wit and disarming smile from the minute they met and exchanged their first words.

Over the next few days she had shown him all the best places in Douglas, she had taken him home to meet her parents and little by little during their trips out, on buses, trains and trams they'd fallen for each other in a way that seemed unbelievable. Though her friends, and even her parents, hinted that their relationship was unlikely to last, Hilary believed differently and up till only three days ago she had been sure that nothing could destroy their romance.

Hilary inhaled desperately, fighting back tears again. She mustn't cry any more. If she looked weepy when she got to the office Mr Colquitt would comment and she would feel even worse. The elderly office clerk seemed always on the look-out for reasons to criticise her as it was, yet it was almost impossible not to cry. This weekend should have been so fabulous, yet now, looking back, she just felt it had been one long disaster.

The day of Leo's arrival Hilary had been so excited she could hardly breathe. She got to the pier far too early, though the ferry wasn't due in till three o'clock, by two fifteen she was already overlooking the

81

King Edward Pier, in her new blue 'Biba' style mini dress and a new jacket from the Mic Mac Boutique. She had danced excitedly about the rooftop viewing area for three quarters of an hour, gazing at the Isle of Man ferry inching across the azure sea towards her. By the time the boat was tied up and Leo had stepped off the gangway, searching the crowds for her, she was beaming so hard she felt she might burst with joy. She'd battled her way towards him, through the disembarking passengers and had thrown herself into his arms in an ecstasy of happiness.

"Hey, hey," Leo fended her off, holding her at arm's length, laughing down at her. "I'm a fragile Liverpool lad, remember? Watch me suit!"

Leo was even more handsome than she remembered, his blonde hair just like Adam Faith's, his eyes a gorgeous fathomless blue. When he leaned down and their lips met Hilary felt she might die with happiness.

"So, babe, I'm here at last," Leo murmured into her ear, when he finally released her.

"I'm so glad," Hilary breathed tremulously, noticing again the lovely way Leo's eyes crinkled when he smiled, an involuntary action that made her insides go to marshmallow.

"Let's move," He'd said, beaming at her, picking up his bag with one hand while curling his other arm about her waist. They'd strolled slowly through the meeting and greeting crowds, Hilary's heart beating madly, Leo's face a picture of content. As they passed the Sea terminal café and a blast of The Beatles 'Love me do' enveloped them, their lips met again, sealing a memory to last for ever.

Looking back, Hilary now viewed that blissful brief walk along the prom as the pinnacle of Leo's visit. What came after, well, it all went downhill, and now he was gone, most likely never to return. Why should he, when he had thousands of Liverpool girls to choose from with their big store fashions and their Cavern ways?

Hilary paused at the foot of the hill while a bus passed. The roar of it and the blast of diesel fumes made her eyes smart and her nose tickle. "If Mr Colquitt comments on my appearance I'll say it's hay fever," she sniffed miserably. "He can hardly object to that."

Hilary hurried across the harbour footbridge and sped into the narrow lanes back of Lord Street. Hilary knew this area of the town like the back of her hand. Last year she'd taken a secretarial course at the former Hanover Street School and now she was working as a typist in a lawyers' practise, on Athol Street, a short climb up from the harbour.

Hilary's parents owned one of the shabby Victorian boarding houses on Loch Promenade. Hilary had always lived on the prom, and liked being near the shops of Strand Street, the cinemas and all the business of the town. Though recently she'd begun to realise that Douglas didn't look as smart as when she was younger and some areas were looking quite run down. There was a fair amount of demolition going on in the old Victorian town too. She'd been slightly ashamed of Douglas last year, seeing it through Leo's eyes, though he'd seemed not to notice.

"It's like a toy-town," he'd grinned, "compared to Liverpool. It's really gear."

Hilary couldn't really feel insulted. Douglas was still a lovely place, with its two mile long promenade and a bay that was in ways as glamorous as Naples, or so she'd been told.

"If only Leo had come a week later," she panted fretfully as she climbed Station Hill. "If only…" She heaved a sigh. "What's the use? He didn't, and so…" As she turned into Athol Street, which was very much the legal quarter of the town, with its many high narrow buildings, filled with offices, a couple of banks and a newspaper printing works. Hilary smoothed her hair and took a few deep breaths, as she fought against the tide of soberly dressed men and women, all intent on getting to their workplaces on time. Hilary hoped her eyes were not too pink still. The practise receptionist had a condescending manner towards junior staff and Hilary hated going past her desk.

When she'd been taken on, after a stiff interview, at the Legal practice, Hilary's family had been thrilled. "You'll never be out of work in Athol Street," Dad had beamed and Mum had made a special fruit cake for a celebration tea. Hilary, barely seventeen and yearning for more excitement than working in a lawyers' office for the rest of her life wasn't quite so taken by their point of view, but she liked the prospect of earning a good salary and being able to contribute to her keep. She knew Mum and Dad hadn't found the last few seasons easy. Lots of folk were choosing continental destinations rather than holidaying in the Isle of Man. Hilary's friend Sally had recently gone with her parents to Torremolinos, and she'd said it was wonderful.

Hilary didn't envy Sally; Hilary had to be careful in the sun, with her pale, freckled skin, but the thought of warm seas and sangria was certainly exciting, more exciting than their regular family holidays, visiting relations in Cumbria in the dull days of autumn.

The week before Leo's visit Hilary had day dreamed that maybe sometime in the future, when she was eighteen perhaps, Mum and Dad might let her go away with Leo to somewhere exotic.

"Some hope." Hilary heaved a despairing sigh as she came to the shining brass plaque of the solicitors' chambers and pushed open the door. As the musty, floor polish scents enveloped her, her insides quivered. She was still nervous of this grown up world, frequented by wigged and gowned lawyers from the Court House nearby, and where anxious clients huddled in the waiting rooms, sometimes in tears.

Though today the muted, stuffy atmosphere somehow suited her mood, and as there was always a pile of conveyances waiting to be typed on a Monday morning Hilary hoped that working through these documents might prove distracting.

She hurried past the formidable Mrs Dene, that day dressed in a startlingly green Paisley patterned two piece outfit. "Yes, of course, Minister, Mr Kelly will ring you, pront-o!" She was trilling into the telephone, barely glancing at Hilary as she slipped through the reception area.

"Good morning, Miss Cannell," Mr Colquitt barked, as Hilary slipped into the office.

"Good morning," she murmured, taking off her suadette jacket. Hanging it up another pang smote her. She'd saved for weeks for that jacket, wanting to show Leo that Isle of Man girls could also be fashionable. She remembered Leo's admiration as he'd helped it off with it, as they'd got home, and his comment as to how nice it was. That was before, of course, when they had no idea what might ensue...

"Daydreaming won't get your work done, Miss Cannell," Mr Colquitt rapped.

Hilary flushed, took the cover off her typewriter, pulled the top folder towards her and opened it. She inserted a sheet of paper into the sturdy Remington machine, adjusted it and poised her fingers over the keys. She began.

Hilary enjoyed typing. She had been taught well, and rarely needed to look at the keyboard. Her nimble fingers rapidly transferred the ponderous legal jargon onto the foolscap sheets. Mr Colquitt returned his attention to his ledgers, Hilary's shoulders relaxed a little and she tried to push all the unfortunate happenings of the weekend away.

It was no good of course. Even as she concentrated with half her mind the other half was still reeling at the series of misfortunes that had dogged Leo's visit.

The first evening had started so well. Leo had made a favourable impression with her parents and Mum said they could eat in the dining room with the guests. Mum had cooked a lovely dinner and Dad had served them a bottle of Blue Nun wine, which made Hilary feel quite grown up. Soon her head was swimming, with wine and happiness, as she and Leo caught up on all the things they'd not told each other in their letters and phone calls. Outside on the promenade the horse trams clopped by, dusk fell and faintly the strains of 'Love me do' filtered in from a Strand Street pub.

"I can't believe I'm here," Leo said, over coffee, his hand creeping across the table to hers.

"Neither can I," Hilary said tremulously. "Shall we walk along the prom after?"

Leo's grip tightened and Hilary's insides quaked with love.

Then a door banged, running feet approached. The dining room door burst open.

"Cissie's baby is on its way. She's been taken to hospital," Joan Cannell gasped. "You'll have to look after the kids, Hil, they're on their own."

Hilary felt as though a bucket of cold water had been thrown at her. "But Mum…"

"I'm sorry, love, there's no one else. We're expecting visitors off the Dublin boat. Go on, get a move on. Leo won't mind, will you, Leo?"

"No, Mrs Cannell." Leo nodded. How could he say otherwise?

'Full of politeness, that lad is,' had been Dad's verdict when he met Leo last year. Mum had thought so too. But they shouldn't have taken his politeness and good nature for granted. Hilary winced, as two of her typewriter keys jammed and she had to untangle them before she could continue.

That had been just the start of the nightmare. She and Leo had rushed to the King Street flat where Aunt Cissie lived, along with her five children, and Uncle Ernie, when he was home, which wasn't often as he was in the Merchant Navy.

"Oh, you've finally come," Mrs Elliot, a neighbour, opened the door to their knock, a screaming toddler in her arms, and an uproar behind her that made it difficult to make out what she was saying. "I can't hang about. Harold's due for his supper and he'll play merry whatsit if it's not ready." She'd thrust the child into Hilary's arms and stalked off.

There were four more little Skillans in the flat, all in various states of undress and all wailing. Hilary administered hugs, bread, jam and hot milk to all and after an hour she'd got most of them to bed. The littlest, Thomas, just wouldn't be put down and at nine o'clock he was still gazing at them with anxious eyes as they sat together on the sagging sofa.

"What do we do now?" Leo said, not exactly grumpily, but Hilary realised he was put out. And so he might be. He had been cried on, sat on, and had a jammy stain on his new-looking stylishly narrow trousers. "Do you have to stay here all night?"

"Heavens, I don't know." Hilary sighed. "I'm hoping Mum or Dad will come soon and one of them will stay."

"Good," Leo smiled, taking her hand. "Then we'll have the next couple of days to ourselves."

"Yes," Hilary agreed, though she had a horrible foreboding that this wouldn't happen either. If Mum or Dad were looking after the children then she would have to help at the boarding house, with the breakfasts, the cleaning and more than likely serving the evening meals.

A quiet tap at the door announced Joan Cannell's arrival. "I am sorry, love. The boat was late and I had to give them supper. You get off now. Have a nice walk back." She gave Hilary a meaningful look, as if to say 'behave yourself.'

Hilary had no intention of misbehaving. Besides, after a close encounter with five young children suddenly the thoughts of romance and marriage did not seem quite so enticing.

"Are all your family like that?" Leo asked, as they sauntered along the quay.

"Of course not," Hilary said, thinking that just last night if she'd envisaged walking along here with Leo she'd have been in raptures. Somehow, after the chaos of her little cousins and their chaotic home the gleaming water and the reflections of the streetlights evoked nothing more than relief to be somewhere quiet.

"Oh Hil," Leo breathed, as they said goodnight on the stairs of the boarding house. "I wish…"

"I know," she'd said, pressing her finger to his lips. "Sleep tight. See you tomorrow." And then she'd dashed up to her attic room, which was too small to be let and which was her personal haven each summer.

A short while later, as she'd gazed at the stars through the skylight she prayed that by the next day things would have sorted themselves out. Otherwise… She hadn't dared think otherwise, it was all too dreadful.

"You're slow today, Miss Cannell. Are you feeling quite well?" Mr Colquitt's rasping voice broke into Hilary's reverie.

"Yes, Mr Colquitt, I'm sorry." Hilary bent her head and attended to her task. It was better not to remember. Nothing had got any better after that evening. The entire weekend had been a constant rush of helping in the boarding house, feeding and tending the little Skillans and snatching quiet moments with Leo.

And then his last evening had come and Mum had been conscience stricken. "Leo's going tomorrow, isn't he? Off you go now and have a good time. We'll cope." She slipped a couple of pound notes into Hilary's hand. "I'm sorry your weekend's been messed up, but I'm relieved Cissie and the baby are safe and well. We can go and see them soon. You'll like that."

Hilary tried her best to smile, she was glad about Aunt Cissie, but the prospect of viewing a new baby didn't evoke any feelings of excitement, it just made her feel a bit weary.

Leo was sitting on the front steps, staring at the twinkling promenade lights. "What are we to do now?" He'd asked, and Hilary's heart had fallen at his expression. He looked as fed up as she was.

"We're to enjoy ourselves," she'd said quietly, threading her arm through his.

"Honest? No other relations needing attention?" He smiled gamely but Hilary felt wretched.

"I'm so sorry," she murmured, and he'd put his arm around her and they'd stared at the sea and the promenade gardens and eventually they got up, crossed the road and strolled along the promenade walkway. When they felt hungry they bought chips from a snack bar near Broadway. Then they'd walked even further and soon they were at the amusement park at Onchan Head. Leo suggested going on the roller coaster and though Hilary enjoyed the thrill of the ride and the closeness of feeling Leo's arms around her the fact that they had so little time left seemed to be lying between them and the lustre of their longed for romantic weekend had well and truly worn off.

They'd walked hand in hand back along the prom, beneath the swinging strings of coloured lights, while the tide crashed onto the shingle on the beach. They stopped in one of the promenade shelters. Hilary had tears running down her cheeks, which Leo kissed away. As Leo comforted her she thought her heart would break. How was she ever going to manage without him?

As she turned the carriage of the typewriter to release the last sheet of the document Mr Colquitt cleared his throat loudly. Hilary glanced at the clock. It was already eleven ten.

"Oh, I must make the tea," she said, jumping up.

"Thank you, Miss Cannell," Mr Colquitt nodded, with a thin smile.

Hilary was surprised. It was the first time Mr Colquitt had ever cast a smile in her direction. Was he all right? Was she looking as bad as she felt? As the kettle boiled Hilary stole a look in the blotchy mirror near the coat hooks. Her skin was pale against her dark auburn hair, and there were grey shadows beneath her eyes, though her waterproof mascara was still mostly on, thank goodness. Hilary pinched her cheeks, sighed, and put an extra spoonful of tea in the pot. "Buck up, Hil," she told herself. "You're no Juliet. This will pass."

Yet as she pulled the top off the milk bottle a tear ran down her cheek, which she rubbed hastily away. Carrying the tea tray back into the office she thrust down the bitter realisation that as many of her friends had predicted a romance such as hers could never last. There might be only a short stretch of the Irish Sea between Douglas and Liverpool, and a daily boat going to and fro, but she and Leo had jobs to hold down and travelling was expensive. They couldn't hope to see each other often. Maybe it was better that this awful weekend had happened. An abrupt end was best.

She would just have to get over Leo that was all. A gulp of hot tea helped for an instant, though as she pictured Leo, maybe even tonight, with another girl, a pang as sharp as a knife turned in her heart.

"Could you type this as a matter of urgency, please, Miss Cannell?" Mr Kelly, the senior partner, laid a file on her desk. "Marilyn has gone off sick; so inconvenient, and this must get off today."

Mr Kelly strode off, not waiting for her reply. Mr Colquitt cast a sympathetic look at Hilary as she put to one side the conveyance she had been typing and wound a fresh sheet of paper into her machine. 'Don't think, just work,' she told herself, as her fingers typed the date and the office reference, for inexplicably the words of 'Love me do' had begun running thorough her mind and she felt the nauseous pang of loss already invading her heart. It was over, and she must resign herself to the fact.

Instead of going out at lunchtime Hilary ate her sandwiches at her desk and typed on.

Five o'clock came at last. With a feeling of numbness Hilary pulled the cover over the typewriter, turned off the desk light and reached for her jacket.

"Good night, Miss Cannell," Mr Colquitt murmured abstractedly. He was still at his desk, papers strewn about him.

"Good night, Mr Colquitt," Hilary replied, wondering whether the grey haired clerk had any sort of life away from the office. "'See you tomorrow."

"Yes, indeed. Have a pleasant evening." Again Hilary was favoured with a tight little smile as she slipped out, darted past Mrs Dene and hurried into the open air. Well, even if her private life was at a calamitous downturn it seemed she must have proved herself at work seeing as Mr Colquitt's attitude had changed towards her.

Hilary breathed in the sharp gorse scents blowing down from the hills behind the town, glad suddenly to be free of the office and its musty air. A little way ahead she spied a friend amongst the throng of emerging office workers. Usually she would have run to join Jenny Kinnon, but Jenny would have wanted to hear about her weekend with Leo and that was the last thing she wanted to talk about, so as she passed a lane, she turned into it and was soon walking down Victoria Street towards the prom.

Hilary dodged the traffic at the Jubilee clock and strode briskly along the prom, gazing at the sparkling sea. Leo would be home now, maybe he would be writing her a letter, thanking her for the weekend but saying that maybe it would be better if...

Better if...

"No, no, I can't bear it." Hilary dashed across the road before Howard Street, narrowly missing being run down by a horse tram. She wanted to hide away in her quiet attic room. She wanted to be alone, to think, to remember, to grieve...

She pushed open the glassed front door and stepped into the familiar hallway with a scent of braising steak wafting from the kitchen.

"Hilary, is that you? You'll never believe what's been delivered."

Hilary was already on the stairs. She turned, reluctantly and dragged herself along the passage to the kitchen.

"Look!" Her mother stepped out from behind a ribbon tied bouquet of red roses. "These came from Hotchkiss's just ten minutes ago, and they're for you!"

Hilary's heart thumped. This must be Leo's kindly way of breaking up.

"Well, aren't you going to read the card? My, that boy must think a lot of you. Interflora flowers cost the earth."

Shakily Hilary undid the tiny envelope, the writing on the card blurring before her tearful gaze.

"What does it say? Oh Hil, buck up." Mum took the card from her and stared at it. "Love me do!' That's all. What does that mean?" Oh, there's something printed on the back – here, you look."

Hilary gazed disbelievingly at Leo's message, printed in a spidery hand by the florist.

"You must visit my relations some time! I'm thinking of applying for a job in Douglas. Would you like that? All my love, Leo."

Hilary sat down, buried her head in the pepper sweet roses and began to sob, with sheer happiness.

"Oh Hil," Mum took the card from her and read it. Then she also looked tearful. "I suppose next thing is he'll be saving for an engagement ring. It hardly seems five minutes since you were a babe in arms, just like Cissie's newest."

Hilary smiled blearily, her nose crinkled; she sneezed, not once, but twice and then again. "Oh Mum," she wailed, "I'm so happy," she sneezed again, "I've never been so happy, and the flowers are gorgeous," she sneezed again, "but I can't believe I've never told Leo about my hay fever!"

THE BLUE PINAFORE
or
BEN Y THIE

Cornaa

In my first volume of Manx short stories, Climbing to Cregneash, 'The Long Walk' appeared. The tale of a young couple's betrothal, set on the beach between Port Lewaigue, Ballure and The Queen's Pier, Ramsey, a favourite area of mine for walks when I lived in the north in the nineteen eighties and nineties.

Now Alice and William are married and settled at in their first home near Cornaa. Life is idyllic; at least it might be, were it not for 'Grandmother in Law.'

My model for this indomitable woman is my paternal Grandmother, May Corlett of Ballaugh. Nana was a doughty cheerful country lady, a skilled needlewoman, an accomplished cook, a keen member of the Mother's Union and supporter of every church and social event in the district. She was always well turned out, with smart coat and toning hat, the latter securely pinned by one or more fearsomely sharp hat pins.

Alice Kneale pegged the last sheet on the line, tucked her blue pinafore into the sash of her dress and leapt onto the five-barred gate. Aware of a robin watching her from a nearby rowan tree Alice smiled as she stared across the fields towards the sea. Shading her eyes against the sun she could she could just see the tip of Queen's Pier at Ramsey peeping out beyond the headland. At the other end of the pier, on the steps leading to the beach William had proposed, less than a year before.

Now all the fuss, excitement and joy of the wedding was but a warm memory, she and William were settled at Cornaa, in a snug cottage adjoining a scatter of fields for which William held the tenure. She was a responsible married woman, with stature in the community, and as such should have been utterly content.

Which she was - almost. William was the kindest, most considerate husband any girl could wish for. Alice gave thanks, every day, for her good fortune. If only she didn't have two burgeoning anxieties which kept waking her in the small hours, despite the comfort of Will's warm body close beside her.

"Worry solves nothing," she reminded herself sternly. "How often did Mother tell me that?" Yet still she felt a nagging anxiety under her ribs which this morning was more worrisome than ever.

Alice brushed her eyes with the back of her hand. One worry, she trusted, would be resolved in God's good time. What right had she to fret on that score? She and William longed for a family, her dearest hope was to have started a child by now, and surely soon…

But the other worry, well, she could not imagine how any amount of time would resolve that permanent impediment to her happiness.

Alice gazed longingly towards the erect figure of William behind the plough horse in a distant field. He caught sight of her and raised his arm. She smiled and waved back enthusiastically. She should not allow dismal thoughts to fret her; many a woman would envy her luck in capturing the heart of William Kneale.

Temporarily light hearted once more Alice leapt from the gate and hurried back to the cottage, shooing the clucking chickens from her path. She mustn't burden William with her anxieties. No, she must be brave and grownup, and learn to take for granted that though most of her life was perfect there would never be harmony between herself and her intractable grandmother in law!

Alice picked up the last few items of washing. She enjoyed feeding the linen through the heavy rollers of the new mangle; an excellent machine that William had picked up at a farm sale.

"Just the best cloth and I'm finished," Alice sighed with relief. Washday was always tiring. As she shook out the white tablecloth her mouth fell open in horror. The formerly pristine length of pure white damask, presented by William's Grandmother on the day of their betrothal, was streaked with blue stains.

"Oh no," Alice wailed.

She had been so careful; she had taken such pains to tease out a blackberry jam stain, which had occurred at William's birthday tea a week before. She'd soaked the cloth for several days and this morning before its wash it had been perfect.

"I can't understand it," she said frantically. "I treated it so particular."

She peered closely at the stains and then her cheeks reddened as she looked down at her new, blue pinafore. "Oh no!" The front of her pinafore was sodden. She'd been so busy she'd not noticed. The colour must have run from it!

"You must have that blue pinafore, Alice," William had declared at the Saturday market the previous week. "It's the very colour of your eyes." He'd called over the market trader before Alice could caution him.

William was always generous, and the pinafore was pretty, but Alice's experience as a draper's assistant told her at first sight that the pinafore was not of the best quality. She had fully intended to wash the garment before using it. But she hadn't, and this was the result. The dye from it had got onto Grandmother's precious gift.

Alice felt like weeping; indeed tears had already sprung to her eyes. Of all things to happen, just when she was trying to think of some way to get into the old woman's good books, she'd committed this heinous sin. For that was how the old woman would regard it.

"That cloth needs careful lookin' after," Grandmother had said sourly, at the birthday tea, when the jam spoon had fallen onto the cloth.

"Yes, Grandmother," Alice had agreed immediately, though it had been William who had been careless. He'd laughed the matter off and things were just getting back to normal when she'd dribbled tea from the pot as she poured out Grandmother's third cup. If it hadn't been for Grandmother in law they would have been using the small brown teapot that didn't drip, but Grandmother in law drank gallons of tea.

"Give it here, darlin' girl." William had come to her rescue, lifting the heavy teapot as though it was featherweight, and with scones and sweet words he'd jollied his grandmother out of her crankiness and the stains on the cloth had been forgotten.

Though by the time Grandmother left Alice was exhausted. "That was one of the longest afternoons of my life," she'd confided to William, who had laughed and kissed her till she felt better.

"And now!" She sniffled miserably, gazing at the stained cloth. "Now Grandmother in law will probably be so cross she'll never visit us again."

Despite her gloom, Alice smiled. No, that would be too much to hope for."

She ran clean water into a bowl and carefully lowered the tablecloth into it. She shook some salt in, hopefully, and a little bicarbonate of soda. She left the cloth to soak and then went out to hang up the rest of the washing.

Somehow the day didn't seem as glorious, though the sun was still shining and the robin flew again onto the washing line as if to say hello.

Alice stared across the fields. She wished William would return. But he wouldn't be back for hours. He had his mid-day snack with him and on these long days he worked till the light faded. It would be hours before she could confess to him about the cloth.

Alice glanced idly at the track leading to the village as she turned back towards the cottage, pressing her stomach with her fingers, for she felt slightly queasy. Probably panic and hunger, she decided. It was near mid-day and she'd been up since dawn. She would have a bite to eat and then she would walk to the neighbouring farm to collect the milk. She'd intended to go earlier. It was one of her regular chores but the washing had put her behind. It would be grand when William had his own cows and he could teach her to milk them. Alice smiled. William had great plans. One day William would probably have the biggest farm in the north of the island.

Alice blinked. As she'd glanced up the lane she'd thought she saw a stooped figure standing at the turn; a figure that had suddenly disappeared into the shadows shed by the overhanging trees. The person had looked awfully like William's Grandmother. It couldn't be, surely?

Alice peered intently. No, the lane was empty - she must have imagined it. Unless someone was resting on the old churn stone, the first opportunity for a sit down on the long uphill walk from Cornaa.

Alice's heart hammered. Surely Grandmother in law could not have walked all this way? When William had taken the trap to fetch her for his birthday tea the round trip had taken him almost an hour.

Alice swung round, wondering whether she should alert William. No, he was too busy, and she was more than likely mistaken. But what if it was Grandmother and she was resting, girding her bad tempered loins, so to speak, before visiting unexpectedly?

Alice raced to the cottage, tearing off her pinafore. She flung it into the scullery and heaved the bowl with the soaking tablecloth in there too, quickly pulling the curtain across the doorway. She beat up the cushions on the settle and the fireside chair. The fire was blazing heartily and the peat and log baskets were full. Alice was glad that yesterday she had shone the brass candlesticks and dusted every surface.

She plucked her shawl from its peg and closed the front door, shooed the chickens away from the gate and set off down the lane, swinging the milk pail. With luck there would be no one there. It had probably been her mind playing tricks. Then she could carry on to collect the milk. She might bake a batch of scones for William's tea when she returned. That would please him. William had lately admitted that her scones were even better than his Grandmother's.

Alice's tipped boots rang along the stony lane. Her throat tightened as she neared the recessed gateway where she thought she'd seen the figure. She was so prepared to believe that no one was there that her heart banged painfully beneath her ribs when she saw that she had been right all along.

Grandmother in law was slumped against the milk churn ledge looking whey faced and ill, not her usual straight backed bad tempered self at all. At the sight of Alice the old woman showed a grudging appearance of relief though her mouth stayed tight shut.

'Any other body might smile,' Alice thought forebodingly, as she clanked down her pail. "Grandmother, what are you doing here?"

"Come to pay a visit, and why shouldn't I?" The old lady rasped. "I got a lift and thought to walk from the village, but it's farther than I remember." She glared at Alice as though it might be her fault that the road was so long.

"Oh. You must be weary." Alice stood uncertainly. "I was on my way for milk, but shall I walk you to the cottage first? Can you make it now you've had a rest?"

"I'll be needin' to, won't I? You'll not be able to carry me, will ye?"

Alice smiled weakly. "No, but I can give you my arm, Grandmother. Here, lean on me and we'll soon be by the fire."

"Wastin' your fuel on a good day like this? There's a long winter ahead, ye know."

"Yes, but William likes me to keep a good fire burning to drive the damp from the cottage. It stood empty for two years before we took it."

"I know, I know. Cissie Corlett was Ben y Thie and she and her boy, Ffinlo lived there until they moved to Rhumsaa."

Alice said nothing, but gave the old lady her arm. Once the old lady started referring to things in the Manx Alice knew better than to chatter for there would be no pleasing her. Ben y Thie, indeed;

Woman of the House. Alice's cheeks dimpled involuntarily. She supposed she was Ben y Thie now.

They soon reached the cottage. Alice shooed the chickens away and pushed open the door. "There now, sit and rest, Grandmother. I'll put the kettle on the fire and by the time I am back with the milk it will be boiled."

"Hrumph!" The old lady muttered, but she sat willingly enough in William's fireside chair, her hands shaky as they rested on the wooden arms.

"Will you be all right? Shall I call William?"

"I'll be right enough," the old lady flapped her hand dismissively. "You be gettin' the milk, chile,' I'll rest here."

Alice swung the kettle onto the hob, gave her a tentative smile and ran from the cottage. She hared down the lane, her heart pounding faster than her feet. May Quine's farmstead was deserted, but Alice scooped milk herself from the churn in the outhouse into her pail and was soon on her way home. Only as she let herself into the cottage did she remember the tablecloth soaking in the scullery. If Grandmother had been snooping she would have found it.

Along with a feeling of dread Alice suddenly felt queasy. She hurried into the scullery and laid down the milk pail. She pressed her middle for a moment and took a few deep breaths.

"This kettle's singin' fit to burst," Grandmother croaked.

Alice forced a smile and emerged with the teapot. "You're feeling better?" She asked as she warmed the pot and then spooned in plenty of tea.

"Aye," the old lady replied, but Alice noticed that she still looked pale and her fingers were shaky undoing the buttons on her coat.

"A cup of tea will make us both feel better," Alice said. "I'll fetch the milk." In the scullery again queasiness overcame her. She tried to hold it back but it was difficult to scoop the creamy milk into the jug without smelling it and the smell almost made her retch.

Clenching her teeth Alice returned to the kitchen, poured a cup of tea for Grandmother and handed it to her. Then she poured a cup for herself but added no more than a splash of milk.

"What's amiss, girl? You like your tea milky, I thought?"

"M'm," Alice said, through clenched lips. She took a sip, and after the first awful moment the hot tea actually made her feel better.

Grandmother's hand shook as she lifted her cup to her lips.

"Can you manage? You're not well, are you?"

"I'm all right. As good as I can hope fer at my age."

Alice said nothing. She wished she'd signalled to William to come home. The old lady clearly had an ulterior motive in this unexpected visit and Alice knew she lacked William's ability in dealing with the old lady's irascible moods.

Alice looked up, just as the old lady did too. Their eyes met warily. Alice tried to look away but the old lady's gimlet stare held hers. Alice felt as though something awful was about to happen. She thought of the cloth in the scullery and her face suffused with colour. Then a totally unexpected thing occurred.

Grandmother smiled.

Not a particularly reassuring smile. Certainly not a beaming smile. But a resigned smile, a grudging smile – almost of defeat.

Alice panicked. Now what was going to happen? Grandmother in law had never smiled at her before. Not even on their wedding day – in fact that day she'd been in such a surly mood William had not got the benefit of a smile either.

"You got me beat, young lady."

Alice swallowed hard, the queasiness returning.

"I thought I'd better come, seeing as the dray man offered me a lift. Lately I've been feelin' bad."

"Oh, shall I fetch William. I'm sure he'll be most concerned if you're ill."

"No, no, not that sort of bad." the old lady's hand flapped her bloodless fingers impatiently. "My goodness, girl, let a body get her words out."

"Sorry. Sorry, Grandmother in law," Alice said meekly.

"I've been feelin' bad because I've not taken to you the way William thinks I should have."

"Oh!" Alice exclaimed.

"I couldn't bear it, at first, you takin' William from me," the old lady's eyes looked into the fire. "That boy's been all to me."

Alice nodded. She knew how the old woman had reared William since his parents were taken by the influenza when he was a tiny baby.

"I didn't think any woman'd be good enough for him," she said, jutting out her chin defensively, as though Alice might rebut this suggestion.

Alice nodded again. "I see."

"I thought you might be flighty. Might let him down."

"Oh, Grandmother, I'd never do that. William and I – well we..." Alice shrugged. Some things could not be put into words. Some things were too precious to speak about. .

"I know. I saw it last week when I was here." The old lady's head drooped. "It was a good birthday tea you gave him. You're a grand cook, Alice Kneale, maybe better than me. An' you keep your home real nice."

Alice felt tears welling behind her eyes. If her own Grandma had praised her like this she'd have hugged her. But this was Grandmother Kneale and somehow, somewhere, there'd be a barb at the end of all these compliments, she just knew it.

"I'll have another cup of tea, mebbe, an' a slice of bread an' butter." The old lady held out her cup. Her hand shook so that only Alice was quick the cup would have fallen to the floor.

"I'm not feelin' quite myself," the old lady admitted, resting her head back. "But you'll not call William. We'll sit and have a chat an' you can tell me what brand of a chile' you're hopin' for."

Alice slopped tea into the saucer. "What?"

"The ailin' - I saw it in your face when you were takin' your tea. It's natural enough, an' it'll probably mean you're havin' a girl." Grandmother's faded eyes gleamed. "But you'll not want to name the babbyn after me, will ye?"

"Grandmother in law! Honestly! Is this really your business?" Alice's heart pounded. Could the old lady be right? She'd felt queasy off and on for days but thought she'd overdone the cream at William's birthday.

A crabbed smile crept over Grandmother's face. "That's more like it. That's the first time you've answered back, Alice Kneale, and about time too!"

100

Alice gaped. She could not get over the old woman's cheek. How dare she speak to her like this! How dare she?

Then she saw a tear creep out from the Grandmother's eye and realised what sheer strength of character it must have taken to come here and effectively admit to being in the wrong.

No wonder she wasn't feeling well. Poor old woman.

Alice rushed to the bread crock and drew out the loaf.

"A slice of my good bread will make you feel better, Grandmother in law," Alice declared, slicing and buttering the bread with the swift sure movements of youth, and cutting the slice into neat tri-angles. "And then, Grandmother, I need your help. I've had a mishap today, with the lovely tablecloth you gave us."

Alice waited for the explosion, but it didn't come.

She turned, the plate of bread and butter in her hand.

Grandmother was asleep, her mouth hanging open.

"Thank goodness," Alice whispered, "What was I thinking of? One thing at a time, my girl."

She lay the plate down, tiptoed to the scullery, plucked up her damp pinafore and slipped out of the cottage into the bright sunshine. She hurried towards the five-barred gate. Taking great care Alice climbed to the next to the top rung and then, holding on securely with one hand, she raised the pinafore above her head, and whirled it round and round.

Almost immediately William noticed, he dropped the horse's reins and began to run towards her, loping effortlessly over the newly turned soil.

Seeing this Alice threw the pinafore high in the air - a cornflower blue spiral against the deeper blue of the late summer sky.

"Oh William, William, I've got such news!" She laughed as he came near. William's white teeth flashed with a smile that made her heart race.

By the time they were in each other's arms the pinafore had fallen among the chickens. The plump, well fed birds clucked and trampled it with muddy inquisitive claws, but William and Alice were too engrossed to notice.

THE RAIN FELL

Peel

Sometimes I despair of the modern world - constant traffic – always speeding too fast – even in our small island - mothers with prams glued to mobile phones instead of enjoying lively, confidence building chats with their children

I fear for the well-being of the millions of men, women and young folk whose minds seem constantly on consumables and 'must haves' who, over the past few years, have become inseparable from technology. Yes it is wonderful to be connected and yes it is convenient, but humankind was not meant to be continually 'on line' or 'on call.' If the next generation is as increasingly dependent on these sophisticated technological 'dummies' what inner resources will they ever develop? They will be too frightened to leave their homes without a personal satnav.

I fear too for our planet: the recent cataclysmic weather variations caused or not by global warming, should be a signal to all governments that something is seriously amiss and needs urgent remedy. That the arctic ice is melting at an alarming rate is an incontrovertible fact.

When will the superpowers take stock and insist that the ever escalating production of consumer inessentials to feed the vanity and ever hungry maw of humanity is reduced? Energy for production results in atmospheric pollution. What use are all these 'things' if we cannot safely breathe?

This is a light hearted take on an unsettling theme, undoubtedly personally biased, and hopefully unlikely.

The rain fell all night. Sandra Callow stirred a few times, but lulled by George's steady breathing and the cosy warmth of his body she soon dropped off again, tired from the busyness of Christmas Eve yet buoyed up, each time she came to consciousness by a warm glow of satisfaction. Everything she had listed on her fridge magnet notebook - bought in the summer from The Home of Rest for old Horses on Richmond Hill – had, this year, been ticked off. This Christmas Day, the first in their new Ballawattleworth home, was going to be a success. She was ready for anything.

The happening, when it occurred, and much of the world barely noticed it, was unremarkable. The steady rain ceased, the temperature plummeted and soon after there was a shower of substantial hailstones. These drummed on roofs and splashed into rivers and oceans; they cooled tropical forests and clattered into glacier corries and icy ravines. It was a brief shower, unlike the incessant heavy summer rains of the past five years, it lasted less than an hour, but it fell over all the regions and oceans of the world.

'A shower of charged particles,' was how the radio stations decided to transmit the news, at least those Far Eastern broadcasters which continued on air for a short time. The rest of the globe remained in ignorance, even the BBC, until an enterprising radio ham in Hong Kong sent a Morse message tapping across the hemisphere to Dorset where another keen radio buff, called Tom, was gazing perplexedly into the darkness. Tom forwarded the brief message to a fellow buff in central London, known as Inky3. Inky3 scrawled a few words with a stub of pencil on the back of a final demand envelope, and as he had no desire to return to bed, being a habitual insomniac, he clipped his West Highland Terrier, Bert, onto his lead, and plodded to Downing Street where he handed the message to a chilled and gloomy looking police constable.

Sandra meanwhile slept on, as did George, Jeremy and little Pearl, cosy in her cot in the tiny third bedroom, unaware that this, her second Christmas would be one that her parents would not forget.

Jeremy woke first, as is the way with five years olds and not only on Christmas Day. Without reaching to switch on a light he rummaged into his stocking, pulling out sweets and chocolate, unwrapped a toy car, a banjo, then some paints. He kept delving until finally he found his heart's desire, a Tweenie Tots i mp player, promised him by Santa, via Mum and Dad.

Jeremy opened the lid, clicked the switch, waited, frowned, and then roared at the top of his voice. "It don't work!"

Sandra heard his cry and prodded George hopefully. As there was no response, she reached to switch on the bedside lamp, but it did not light. She peered at her bedside clock, an old fashioned wind up variety with luminous figures. Six fifteen. It could be worse, she thought, slipping reluctantly from bed, eager to quell Jeremy before he wakened Pearl. When she pressed the landing light switch and that did not work either she guessed there was a power cut. Her heart beat a little faster, though it was yet too early to dwell on the implications of a cold cooker and a large defrosted turkey. That anxiety could be postponed. Jeremy must be hushed, and now. Feeling her way along the landing she entered her small son's room.

His light didn't work but by now her eyes were accustomed to the gloom. "Happy Christmas, poppet, she said, bending to kiss him. "Hush now, you'll wake Pearl, and we're having a lie in today."

Jeremy held out his i player. "Mummy, Santa's given me a bad one. It don't work!"

"It doesn't work," Sandra said, automatically correcting her son as she peered at the blank screen and clicked the controls. . She handed the player back, frowned, drew one of the giraffe patterned curtains and peered out. The entire district was in darkness, even the house opposite, where the landing light was always left on for the children. Sandra pressed her nose to the corner of the window, staring beyond the estate towards Peel promenade. There were no street lights visible. She sighed "There must be a power cut, honey. There's not a light to be seen." Sandra smiled, while thinking, still rather sleepily that surely the i player should work from its batteries, which had only been inserted the day before. "Never mind," she said, leaning down to scoop Jeremy into her arms. "Come and snuggle in with us till Pearl wakes."

"Don't want to," Jeremy wriggled. "Can I watch TV?"

Sandra's eyesight was now attuned to the grey dimness. She looked at the mess of discarded wrappings from the toys she had so lovingly bought for her son. "What about playing with your other new things?"

"Don't want 'em in the dark. Can I watch Star Wars again?"

"Sorry?"

"Please."

"Jeremy, I just said, there's a power cut. You can't watch anything, poppet."

Jeremy's outraged shrieks echoed around the house. "That's not fair," he yelled, reaching for his new i player and bashing it on the bedhead.

A similar scenario was being played out across the world. Mobile phones were being shaken, banged, then pulled to bits and plugs inserted and reinserted. Switches were clicked fruitlessly, frantically and fearfully. Grown men gaped helplessly at their blank screens, women and girls shrieked and burst into tears. Overall clad men in power stations scurried to and fro, vainly trying to restart their massive machines. In an escalating exercise the door knockers of Supervisors, District Superintendents, Executive officers and then Government Ministers were rattled peremptorily by lesser, or greater minions until the Prime Minister himself, on holiday at Chequers, was, after a couple of hours, contacted by a special branch man on a bicycle sent post haste from MI5 with a message that he was to return to London immediately.

"How do I get there?" the Prime Minister asked crossly, after being informed that all global transport was at a standstill, trains, planes and even cars refusing to move and that the network of mobile phone masts were either dead or of such little use that one might as well resort to semaphore. The official belief so far was that the hail shower had caused an astronomical magnetic surge affecting the entire planet.

The special branch man did not feel like being helpful to the PM. This was the first Christmas Day for years that he'd actually got off. Or thought he had until he'd been woken abruptly by his wife shaking him and saying 'there's someone throwing stones at our window,' and when he looked out it was his boss, in overcoat and pyjamas, beckoning.

"I can't let you have my bike because I'd be stranded then, wouldn't I?" he said tersely, though quite reasonably, he thought. "But I passed a cycle shop in the village about a mile back. Maybe, seeing as it's you, they'll hire you a bike, even if it is Christmas Day."

"Thanks very much," the Prime Minister glared, shutting the door in his face.

"You're welcome, " the special branch man shouted over his shoulder as he jumped on his cycle and rode off. Seeing as he'd had to get up this early he was determined to enjoy the ride back to London. He'd never known the roads so empty.

Meanwhile Sandra and George had got up and were sitting at the breakfast table in their dressing gowns. "What are we going to do? Even Manx Radio isn't working. "

"Well, we can have cereal for breakfast," Sandra said, "but there's no chance of Christmas dinner without the oven."

"Bloody hell," George said. "That turkey cost the earth."

By nine o'clock people most people in the Island were standing outside their houses, gazing at the sky, and at the remains of the hailstones, which lay in a gritty layer across the land. Neighbours, friends and enemies exchanged views, advice and gloomy predictions.

Only around the churches was there any optimism. It was Christmas Day after all and this happening might be the prelude to the Lord's return. What a glorious event that would be, the Saviour coming back at last.

The gathering congregations at the Cathedral in Peel were especially upbeat. The vicar was beaming.

"Though offering Himself tea or coffee after the service will be tricky," regular worshipper Janice Kneen whispered to her friend

Brenda Kaighen, "and the oldies will be uppity, you know how they get without their cuppa?"

"They'll have to show Christian fortitude and do without," Brenda's Dad declared listening in. Brenda and Janice exchanged glances. They both knew that Ewan Christian had the warmth of a bowl of porridge and several cups of hot tea inside him, prepared by his long suffering wife Bella on their old fashioned coal fired cooking range.

"That's not very charitable on Christmas morning, Dad." Brenda said. She frowned for a moment and closed her eyes, trusting in divine inspiration. This came, to her surprise, quite promptly. "I know," she cried. "We bought a tiny fuel camp stove last summer. We can boil a kettle on that." She flung her leg over her bike and headed for Patrick Street.

Meanwhile George was gazing ruefully at the defrosted fourteen pound turkey they had purchased expensively from Shoprite only a few days earlier. "What'll we do with it?" He grumbled, poking it with a fork.

"We'll cook it," Sandra replied, pulling down a roll of foil from the top of the fridge. "Wrap it up well. "I' m going to make a fire pit."

"You are going to do what?" George gaped. Though he was often amazed by his wife's resourcefulness, and regularly startled by her depth of knowledge and innate intelligence, this suggestion sounded outlandish, even for Sandra. "What in heaven's name is a fire pit?"

"Oh, come on, you've watched Bear Grylls and whatshisname? You dig a pit, get a fire going in it and then when the embers are dying you put in what you want to cook and bob's your uncle!"

George gazed at the mound of turkey flesh before him. "Will we catch salmonella?"

Sandra glared. "Yes, if we don't check that it's properly cooked, but we will. Won't we?" She stood arms akimbo, and George wilted under her scrutiny. "Of course we will, love." He took her in his arms and hugged her. "You're so brave, Sandy, I'm scared. Nothing like this has ever happened before."

"I am too," she replied, nuzzling his neck and inhaling the familiar, dearly loved but slightly sweaty scent of him which reminded her that she'd need to do something about heating water for a wash too. "We're not wasting that turkey, I've made my mind up. Yes, the power might come on again before it's done and if so I'll pop it in the oven. But this is our first Christmas in our own home and I want us to have a proper festive dinner. It won't seem like Christmas otherwise."

George kissed her. "Shall I dig a pit then?" He said, without a whit of enthusiasm.

Sandra laughed. "Don't be soft. I don't want you moaning about your back for weeks. I'll dig it in the veg bed. I turned that bit of ground over last month anyway, after I'd lifted the spuds and leeks. It'll not take long. You look after the children. Keep them amused. Oh, and rinse the breakfast dishes the best you can with cold water. "

Sandra was already pulling on a jacket and long socks. George lifted her wellington boots from the under stair cupboard and handed them to her.

"Thanks, petal, oh, and get the children dressed in warm clothes. We might not have any heating today, don't forget."

George felt his chest tighten. He wished he didn't feel so scared. He wished he was the brave, resourceful cave man type that Sandra and the kids deserved; the type that would go and chop down a tree then build a fire and maybe fling a line into the sea to catch fish to cook on it, but he wasn't brave, he never had been. As a teenager he'd made sure he never caught the late bus home from Douglas after the pictures, because he was afraid of what might happen when the drunks got active. As it was, the blank screen on his phone and no telly or radio unnerved him enough. He couldn't cope with much more.

The fact that the whole world was in turmoil, and suffering the same power loss, did not occur to George, his mental vision was limited, by habit, and by choice. He just told himself that probably the House Of Keys had omitted to pay another of the EU taxes, like in 2017, and the power link, from the Isle of Mull, or was it from Anglesey again now, had been switched off.

He went upstairs, found some suitable, and some not really suitable clothing and headed for the children who were squabbling over a push along railway set in the sitting room.

"Daddy, Jeremy hit Pearl," his almost two year old daughter yelped, her face puce with outrage, while her fingers clutched a handful of Jeremy's hair.

"I didn't mean to," Jeremy protested. "She sat on my head."

"Tut, tut," George smiled. "Well that's a shame, but I daresay you asked for it, son."

Pearl smirked and let her brother's hair go. "He did," she crowed. "'My trucks went fastest and he got cross."

George pulled off Jeremy's pyjama top. "Fair do's," he said. "Hey up, poke your arms in here, son, and we'll soon have you warm and cosy."

Jeremy frowned. "Why can't you turn the light on, Daddy?"

"There's a power cut. It'll come on in a bit."

"Who's cut it, Daddy," Pearl asked as he threaded her arms into a t-shirt and fleece.

"Tynwald, prob'ly," he said gloomily. "You know, the EU."

Jeremy stared. "Doesn't Tynwald like Christmas? Doesn't it want me to have fun with my new i player? That's not fair, is it?"

George pulled out a comb and ran it through Pearl's short blonde curls. "When you're both older," he said, "you'll find out, like I have, that life isn't fair, but by then you'll be able use your vote, or maybe stand for the Keys. What do you think of that?"

The two children regarded him doubtfully. "Mum says all parliaments are cor-rupt." Jeremy frowned. "That's bad, isn't it?"

Pearl nodded her curly head. "Mum said."

George winced. Why did his children always remember what Sandra said? They never remembered anything he told them. George pretended he hadn't heard their question.

"Come on, your mother's digging a pit; let's see how she's getting on."

"A pit!" Jeremy cried. "You mean a big hole? Can I help?"

"And me," echoed Pearl.

"Why's she digging it?"

"She's going to bury the turkey."

Pearl looked shocked, and then began to wail. "That's not fair. Turkey won't like that."

George swung Pearl into his arms. "Turkey's for our dinner, lovey. "Turkey expects to be cooked."

"Yes," Jeremy grinned. "Turkey's dead, isn't he Daddy? He's never going to say 'Gobble, Gobble again."

Pearl's wails increased. George patted his daughter's back and hurried through the kitchen towards the garden. Not for the first time he wondered about the wisdom of fathering children. God, what would he do without Sandra?

The sun rose, and very gradually the layer of grey hailstones melted, leaving a thick ashen dusting over the entire world. By this time men with Geiger counters and all manner of complicated calibrating machines were testing the lying particles and exclaiming with horror at the levels of dangerous magnetism covering the planet, the levels registered were of such magnitude that it was impossible for motors of any type to function.

Grave faced governments met in dim rooms or in the open air, no one as yet having got any source of light to work save candles and even they flickered in the febrile atmosphere.

"We should put out health warnings," a posse of men in charge of such matters shouted to each other.

"What use are health warnings?" Groups of academics riposted. "If we get another of these showers then life as we know it will just stop."

On the Isle of Man, as news got round that it wasn't an ordinary power cut people stood in the streets and gossiped, waiting and hoping to be told what to do and find out when their mobile phones and central heating would work again. Large gatherings congregated around the Commissioners offices in Ramsey, Peel and Port Erin. In Castletown they gathered in the Square. In Douglas crowds wandered onto the promenade and then headed for Prospect Hill and Government buildings. The gathering multitude were mostly young women, many of them sobbing, clutching their dead phones and crying over them like bereft mothers while the lads, acting cocky, holding back their panic, complained that seeing as they'd voted in this lot of no hope MHKs it was up to them to sort out this fiasco. How could life go on without a mobile, Facebook and Twitter?

There were some older folk too, a scattering of pensioners and divorcees who had nothing better to do, standing bleakly, fingers fruitlessly texting, or cradling their phones to their ears hopefully, just in case.

Yet in many homes people stayed put and tried to make the best of things. These were, in the main, men and women of mature years, who had been brought up to be self-reliant, and who either had never used modern technology or mistrusted it and had lived perfectly happy lives despite such advances. Some of these had never spoken into a mobile phone or only borrowed one when they went 'across.' These folk popped into their neighbours to wish them Happy Christmas and depending on who was better off either stayed or took their neighbours back home. Those with fireplaces soon had their fires blazing and a kettle humming for cups of tea, and 'all electric' neighbours were invited in for a hot drink and maybe a whisky toddy and a mince pie. It was such a special day, after all. Many of these gatherings got quite cheerful discussing plans to cook their own and their neighbours Christmas poultry over the fire. "Like in Grandma's day," they laughed and somehow a sort of blitz feeling was recreated, and everyone felt a little closer and happier, even in this dire emergency.

In Athol Road Peel, one such old lady was full of glee as she got out the old trivet that had stood unused in her front room for years.

"This was our best Sunday trivet," Granny Kermode smiled, placing the kettle on the shining brass stand over the gleaming coals. "Do you remember it, Linda?"

Linda smiled. "I do, Mum. We only used this on special days," she told her children, Flora and Eddy. "Once the kettle started humming we would hold the toast to the fire, wouldn't we Mum?"

"Aye, that's right. We'll soon have this kettle singing and then you children can take turns with this." She handed a shining brass toasting fork to Flora. "You take first turn, Flora, and then give it to your little brother."

"Yes, Granny," Flora replied gleefully, gazing delightedly at the shining prongs while Eddy carefully speared a piece of sliced bread onto the fork.

Linda glanced meaningfully at her husband Gary. He met her look with a chastened expression, as well he might. If they'd had it his way they'd have stayed with his parents again this year. Linda had resorted to bribery to get her way, Gary liked regular cuddles; Linda warned him that all such would be unavailable if they had to spend yet another Christmas with his parents in their super modern home at Tromode. The children were about as welcome there, in its pristine interior, as long tails from the nearby Tromode River. It had been 'don't' touch that' and 'keep off there' all Christmas and Boxing Day last year. Even when the kids went to play in the expensively landscaped garden they had been warned not to step off the paths, while here Flora and Eddy were free to roam all over the house, playing hide and seek, castles and kings or whatever they wanted. Linda settled back in Dad's old rocking chair and felt a surge of pleasure that this year they would have a real old fashioned family Christmas. Whatever had happened in the world didn't really matter - no doubt it would soon get put right, but for now she could relax and know that Mum would take care of them all, and Gary would just have to lump it.

Sandra Callow, meanwhile, had dug a grand fire pit in the garden. It was lucky they'd chucked out an old chest of drawers recently, which had been destined for the amenity site, but hadn't got there. Broken up, and with other bits of rubbish Sandra soon had a good blaze going.

"That's really hot," George said, holding Pearl and Jeremy's hands. "How long before you can cook the bird?"

"I'm not sure," Sandra said, kicking at the layer of melting hailstones with her boot. "They're gritty, aren't they? I wonder what they're made off. Not just water, for sure."

George averted his gaze; he looked over the houses towards Peel Hill and Corrin's Tower. Thank God that at least was reassuringly unchanged. He frowned, listening. Without tellies blaring out or car engine's running the estate was eerily quiet, save for a strange muffled noise. "What is that?"

Sandra shrugged. "People crying because they're disappointed in their Christmas presents, I suppose." She said lightly, and then added. "Why not take the children inside, love? It's cold out here and I'll need to rake out this fire soon. It's going to be messy and there'll be sparks and smoke everywhere."

"Are you sure you can manage?" George asked.

"Absolutely," Sandra smiled, though her face fell as soon as George and the children had gone. That constant sobbing in the background was people unable to cope. She knew it and heavens, her own heart was banging with unease. What had happened wasn't just a blip; she felt it in her bones. It was serious, and the future that she'd looked forward to so much now seemed vague and uncertain. Still, it was good that she had something immediate to focus on. This turkey had to be cooked. Live in the moment that was the way to cope, for now. Sandra raised her spade and began to shovel out the embers.

A few streets away, in one of the narrow Victorian terraced houses in Stanley Road Colin Shimmin was being shaken gently awake by his Dad.

"Happy Christmas, son. Come on now, take note. Your mother thought I'd better rouse you in the circs."

Colin stirred, his hand reached automatically to his bedside table.

"No, lad, listen, there's been a power cut or something. Your radio won't work. Nothing works. 'Don't know why. The phones, the telly, the lot, they're all down. All your stuff, your phones and that, they'll be useless."

"What? You mean there's no music!" Colin burbled, sitting bolt upright, a horrified look on his delicate, rather nervy face. Colin was a second year music student on holiday from the Royal Academy.

"Aye, here's a drink of barley water. Your mother thought you might like it. It'll be a while before things are sorted, I reckon." Jim gazed at Colin with anxious eyes, and then hurried out. Jim always felt ill at ease around his sensitive son. Though he loved him dearly it was as though Colin lived on a different planet. Jim and he customarily

113

treated each other with exaggerated respect, it was hard to believe they were related, such were their differences.

Colin gulped a mouthful of barley water then lay back. Had Dad really said what he thought he'd said? Or was he still in the midst of a dream?

He blinked, no his head was aching. He was awake. He'd drunk too much cider the night before. He'd known it even as he downed that last pint at the Marine, but Chazzer was there and Ben and they'd been...

His fingers reached unwittingly to his bedside table and closed round his phone. Even though he'd taken in Dad's words he was still startled by the look of the dead screen and the fact that when he tried to make it work it wouldn't. He tucked the phone beneath his pillow and reached for his earphones and his music player, surely that must work. It didn't need a telephone mast; it worked off batteries, didn't it?

The earphones felt warm and familiar as he slipped them into his ears. He pressed the usual button, waiting, listening, pressed it again, and again, fruitlessly.

"No!" Colin's heart banged with disbelief. His chest tightened. He had to have music. He needed it like any ordinary man needed food and water. What was life without music? How could he get through a morning, how could he survive a day, even, or more especially, Christmas Day, without music?

Colin glanced at the barley water again. He reached, gulped at it and swung his legs out of the bed in one movement, reaching for his violin case, which was always to hand. He never let Amadeus out of his sight. The instrument, named after the Master himself, was more than just a violin, at times it felt like his other half. If he was away from Amadeus for long, like last night at the pub, for instance, he got sick and stupid with longing, and his imagination plagued him with visions of some disaster happening to it.

Colin clicked open the fasteners, revealing the violin's soft dust cloth cover, the rosin, and the instrument beneath. Reverently he lifted his beloved friend from his resting place. His heart slowed as he raised the instrument to its playing position. He breathed a sigh of pleasure as he eased his chin to the rest and settled onto it. The feel of the violin in its right place, was calming, and the action of curling his fingers about the violin's delicate neck brought forth a smothered smile to his face. Colin lifted the bow and played a scale, then another, followed by a more complicated glissando, forcing the resonance of the notes to linger in the air, mesmerizingly soothing his heart, his mind, his spirit. He walked to the window, flicked back the curtain with his bow and gazed down the hill to the promenade, the sea and the castle beyond.

Equilibrium restored Colin closed his eyes and launched into an uplifting Mozart scherzo, the music filling the house and resounding into the street. Even if all the music in the world had been stilled Colin knew that as long as Amadeus served him he would survive.

Downstairs his parents smiled at each other. James Shimmin patted his wife's cheek. "There," he said, "all's right with our world." Unworried by the power cut they sat in candle light beside the fire and talked of the old days, while a pan of simmering beef stew cooked on the hearth.

"We're hale and hearty; we've got a son with a gift from God. What's to worry about?" Jim murmured to Thelma. She was knitting, yet another square for orphans in Zambia. Over the years Thelma had had put together more than a hundred blankets. It was a simple hobby, but she enjoyed it, and it was useful. "Aye," she smiled, "we'll play musical scrabble later, Colin will like that."

"No letting him win, though Thelma," Jim smiled. "The lad needs to learn to lose."

She chuckled. "We'll see."

The scent of cooked turkey filled the Callow's kitchen with the most delightful seasonal aroma as Sandra unwrapped the many layers of its foil blanket. The turkey looked magnificent, golden, succulent, juice running from it, dripping onto the table.

"It's taken longer than I imagined," Sandra said, tucking the foil up and dabbing at the drips with a dishcloth, before wiping her grubby brow with the same cloth, her fingers blackened, ashy and scorched. " I doubt there's heat enough left for the veg."

George grinned. The two children,   their noses peeking over the table edge at the steaming bird, giggled.

"We've got a surprise for you, Mummy," Jeremy laughed.

"And I helped," Pearl cried.

Sandra washed her hands under the tap. The flow of the water was erratic. She glanced anxiously at George, but he pretended not to notice.

"I'll carve shall I, love?" George said. "You go and sit at the table, you must be exhausted." He handed Sandra a towel. "I saw you chatting to them next door? What was all that about?"

"They called to me. I couldn't believe it. Honestly, they were both in a real dither, scared of walking to their parents' house in St. John's. Scared! A young couple like that. You'd have thought they were a couple of pensioners and not a pair of twenty something's. Anyway, I said I'd keep them some turkey for tomorrow. We'll have loads and it will have to be eaten soon if the power doesn't come on."

"Mummy, mummy. Come and see what we done." Jeremy entreated, pulling her hand.

"What we did," Sandra said automatically, then smiled and allowed herself to be tugged towards the dining room. "All right, what *have* you been doing with Daddy? Surprise me!"

"We will," Pearl giggled, clinging to her skirt.

"Ta-ra!" George said, opening the door to the dining room.

"Wow!" Sandra gasped, while the children giggled and clapped.

The dining room looked magical. The table was laid with cutlery, glasses and Christmas serviettes. There were crackers at the four places and on the two window ledges, table and sideboard candles flickered in the afternoon gloom, closing out the dark and unhappy world beyond.

Filled bowls were set on the Christmas runner in the midst of the table. Sandra gazed at them and then back at her family. "You have been busy. What are all these?"

"Coldslaw!" Pearl cried.

"Coleslaw," Jeremy corrected.

"And Salad, with tomatoes, spring onions and cucumber," George said, beaming.

"Rootbeets too," Pearl said, and they all laughed.

"And crisps," Jeremy added. "'Cause Daddy said we couldn't have hot veggies with the cooker not working."

"Well done, Daddy," Sandra said, throwing her arms about him."

"There's cheese and fruit for pudding," George said, kissing her, and then swinging Pearl into her booster seat. "You've worked so hard with that turkey, all that digging and turning it and so on."

"It was nothing," Sandra shrugged, though her arms were aching and several finger tips were tingling with small burns.

"I'll carve and fetch it in? O.K?"

"O.K." Sandra said, sinking into her chair gladly. "It's taken hours, hasn't it? I don't know where the day's gone. The meat had better not be tough."

It wasn't. A few moments later George returned with a plate piled with thick slices of perfectly cooked turkey. Soon everyone was tucking in.

"I think this is the nicest Christmas dinner I've ever had," George said, when his plate was half cleared.

"Have more," Sandra smiled, pushing the turkey plate nearer. She had determinedly pushed all that needed to be worried about to the back of her mind. The children deserved this peaceful Christmas respite, and so did she and George.

"It's been a Christmas to remember," she said, reaching across and gripping George's hand.

His fingers held hers, their eyes met. Fear of the future lurked behind their easy loving smiles, but they would not give way. Their family was together and for now they were safe and well fed.

George picked up a cracker and held it out to Jeremy.

"Me too," Pearl cried and held her cracker out to her mother.

Outside, once more, the rain fell, and this time, more heavily...

THE CHANGING TIDE

Port Soderick

As children my sister and I relished stormy sea crossings to Liverpool and Belfast. We raced around the decks of the Tynwald, King Orry, Lady of Mann, Ben my Chree or Mona's Isle – we were familiar with all the Steam Packet ships. Heedless of danger we skidded across spray soaked decks and stared over salt coated rails, exhilarated by the excitement of 'going across.' We never travelled First Class, our mother would either settle in the Steerage Ladies Lounge – under the aegis of a starched stewardess, offering maternal care, cushions and rugs, otherwise we would descend to one of the lower lounges, laying claim to a prickly upholstered couch and upper bunk. The upper berth had a sea splashed porthole against which you could press your nose. A compulsory 'rest' against a moquette pillow resulted in an interestingly patterned cheek, though that was soon forgotten as we raced upstairs once more, through the pie scented buffet saloons and out again onto the wind- blown decks. The engine room was a must on every trip; from the barred but open door we could see the huge pistons powering us 'across the water.' Not too long was spent there though for the rising heat was nauseous, mixing as it did with the smell of the nearby lavatories.

In 2006 Billy Stowell of the Nautical Museum, Castletown loaned me a copy of the West Coast of England Pilot, 1933. In reading this fascinating book I discovered a new expression, 'the scend of the sea' which prompted the following story.

118

Matthew Kinrade held the tiller firmly, his heart thumping. The waves on all sides were enormous, higher than he had ever experienced. The wind was a strong northeasterly, the most treacherous direction for sailing off the east coast of the Isle of Man. If he made just one mistake he would be swept onto the jagged rocks beneath the cliffs.

"But I won't make a mistake," Matthew muttered grimly, his lips stinging with salt. "I cannot." His nerve was strong, though the thundering of his heart belied his determination.

Had there been any alternative he would have taken it gladly, but there had been none. Amy needed the mid-wife and the road from their cottage was impassable. This treacherous sea passage was his only hope.

It had wrenched his heart leaving her. He should have gone for assistance sooner. Amy had never been one to fuss, but this time her stoicism might prove to have been a mistake. "Please God, let it not be so," Matthew breathed as he tugged at a rope. Amy had put on such a brave show as he left her but there'd been desperation in her usually merry eyes.

"Don't be long, will you Matt. I'm scared."

"Hardly more'n an hour, darlin' girl. The Nessy will get me there and back in no time."

Matthew ground his teeth as another huge wave threatened his vessel. Brave words, Matthew Kinrade, he thought. Brave, or foolish? His father's warning, spoken on the day he bought the Nessy, swirled through his mind as he fought to maintain control.

"The scend of the sea will not alter on any whim of yours, lad. The tides and winds have been logged by better men than you or I. Take a chance on doing things your way and you'll not see port."

It had been a blunt warning, from a retired seafarer to a novice. His father's admonition had been stern, but there had been pride in his eyes as well. Silas Kinrade knew what it was to be lured by the sea, to feel no contentment save being in sight of the ocean or on it. He did not begrudge his son the life he had chosen, how could he? The sea still held sway in the old man's heart.

That had been three years before, in the autumn of 1933. Those three years had been fruitful for Matthew. He had proved himself a competent and careful mariner, with a good business head besides. His income from fishing and cargo work to Whitehaven had provided the wherewithal to take over a croft beside the sea at Port Grenaugh, a pretty cove popular with tourists. Here Amy intended to set up a tea garden while Matthew hoped that evening fishing trips for holidaymakers might prove a lucrative addition to his regular income.

The couple were young, energetic and full of hope for the future. The expectation of their first child had thrilled them both and Amy had sailed through her pregnancy with ease. She came from a large family; she was well prepared for the birth and not unduly anxious.

But the start of her labour pains had coincided with the greatest storm Matthew could remember. Amy had never liked storms and the sound of the wind roaring round the cottage, the crash of the mountainous seas and the splinter of trees falling in the glen combining with her pains had made her doubly anxious. They had no near neighbours and when ultimately Amy decided she would need the midwife she was torn between sending Matthew to get her and the fact that if she did she would be alone. When she realised he would have to go by sea she pleaded with him not to go. But Matthew was adamant. He was more frightened for her than of the perilous short sea journey.

"Whoa!" Matthew held his breath as a starboard wave almost swamped him. Fighting with a baling tin, the tiller and a sail Matthew felt a twinge of real panic. Perhaps he should have been more frightened. Perhaps this would be the end. Maybe none of their rosy dreams would see fruition. Maybe he'd never see Amy again, or the baby that was putting up such a struggle against being born. Why, oh why had he taken this risk? He should have stayed ashore, to help her, or taken a hatchet to the trees which had lain between him and assistance. That would have been so much wiser.

Matthew grabbed hold of a flailing rope. It burned through his fingers before he had it secure. Yes, but to cut through the trees might have taken half a day. Amy needed help now. On a good sea it would have taken him no more than twenty minutes to reach Port Soderick, where he would be practically within hailing distance of the midwife's cottage.

But this was not a good sea. This was a raging sea, and to be fighting it was madness. Matthew knew in his heart he had gone against his father's advice. If he drowned on this short voyage Silas would be ashamed of him.

"Ugh!" Another ice-cold drench of seawater doused him. Matthew gritted his teeth. Peering through the driving rain he thought he saw a flickering light. This flicker, whether it was real or imaginary made him bale with even more fury and hold onto the tiller with an even tighter grip. He was not going to drown; he was not going to be beaten, by a raging sea, by an inshore wind or by gallons of driving rain. If there was a light abeam he must be near the farm on Santon Head, half way to his goal. Soon he should gain respite because he would be tacking with the wind, instead of fighting it.

Matthew tugged frantically at the sails and moved the tiller to change course. The vessel tossed capriciously as if fighting him.

"Come on Nessy," he cajoled, "You can do it."

He thought at first that he'd pushed her too far. The storm lashed and the rain fell yet the vessel seemed to be barely treading water. And then she had done it. She had turned. The wind was less fierce, the rain, though driving, seemed not the same slanting curtain of ice it had been only moments before. And though the harrying tide swept him towards the rocks even faster now Matthew knew every inch of this coastline and he was in shelter. He was confident that as long as he kept his nerve, with God's help he would soon be home and dry.

The entry into Port Soderick was nonetheless a nightmare. Too late for the hotel to be open for business there was not a jot of light to assist him as he steered his way between a well-known pavement of hidden rocks and the oyster beds to the slim jetty. Only as he drew up did a gleam shine out from the hotel doorway and Jem Stevens, the proprietor come running out.

121

"What the devil are you up to, Matthew?" He shouted over the roar of the wind. "I was on my way to bed and I spied your sail. Are you mad, man?"

Matthew threw a line and Jem speedily tied it round a bollard. Jem held his hand out as Matthew leapt onto the jetty on the rise of a wave. "I had to come, Amy needs the midwife."

"What?" Jem held his hand to his ear. He put his arm around Matthew's shoulders and hurried him to the top of the steps under the canopy that sheltered the hotel. Here the wind allowed them to stand upright though the rain was still driving furiously at their backs.

"I need the midwife for Amy," Matthew repeated, his voice shaky. Now that he had landed Matthew realised how much the short journey had taken out of him. He hardly dared think of the return voyage.

Jem clapped his back. "We'll see if the telephone is working. This storm's played havoc everywhere. There's been floods and trouble all over the island." He hurried Matthew into the warm lobby of the hotel.

The telephone line was dead. "No matter," Matthew shrugged, shaking his wet hair like a dog. "I can leg it up the lane to May Corkish's cottage in moments. "I'll have her back on the boat in an instant."

"You're not thinking of going back by sea?" Jem's eyes widened. "May's terrified of water. She'll not even paddle when she brings her nephew to play here on the beach."

"But we can't go by road," Matthew exclaimed. "The glen road is blocked. We have to go by sea."

Jem stared at Matthew. Then he turned and rushed for his coat. "I'll come with you. I'll maybe have more success persuading May than you."

Matthew couldn't think why he should, but he was glad of the company as they set out in the still torrential rain towards the pair of roadside cottages half way between the port and the railway station. Then in a pause to catch his breath he recalled some tittle tattle regarding Jem and the widowed May Corkish; a rumour that they were walking out together. Matthew cast a wondering glance at Jem. Maybe it was true! If so, Jem must be a brave man, or a fool. May Corkish would be a doughty proposition.

"It looks as if May's still up," Jem shouted. "There's a light in the window, though sometimes she leaves one burning when she's on a call."

Matthew's heart pounded. "What will I do if she's not there?"

"Hold hard, let's find out." Jem hammered on the door. "May, are you in? It's Jem Stevens."

Within moments an upper window slid open. "What are you doing calling at this hour, Jem. Be off with you!"

Jem grimaced. "She's in all right. You take over, young Matthew."

"It's not Jem that's needing you, Mrs Corkish. It's me, Matthew Kinrade. Amy's started and she's bad. We need help."

A curler tight head protruded into the rain. "The door's on the latch. Let yourselves in. I'll be down in two ticks."

Matthew and Jem stepped into the neat living room. The coals of the banked up fire glowed and Matt moved nearer to it. He was a-tremble, though he felt ashamed to be so. It was Amy who was in greater danger than he. What if anything happened? What if...?

"Now what's all this fuss?" Only moments later May Corkish appeared, her stout, well covered frame neatly attired in a grey woollen dress and hand knitted cardigan, with a brooch at her collar. Her greying hair, from which the curlers must have been torn out, so fast had she appeared, was confined under a net so sturdy it could have served to catch herrings. Matthew took in her appearance and suddenly felt easier.

"Amy has been paining for thirty hours," he said, "and she needs you."

"Indeed she must." May went to the corner where a leather bag lay. She picked it up and nodded to Jem, who hurried to the hall and fetched her coat. It was only as he was helping her into it that Matthew added.

"The thing is, we can't go by road. It's blocked. We've got to go back by sea."

123

May's arm, half in a sleeve, faltered. Her face went pale. "By sea? On a night like this?"

"It'll be rough, but not too bad. The tide's on the turn, isn't it, Jem?"

"Is it? Oh aye, it will be."

May gazed at Matthew with horror. "But it's pitch black. I can't." Her lips tightened. "No, it must be better to go by road. You're at Port Grenaugh? That's no distance by car. You'll start the motor Jem won't you? That starting handle fair riles my rheumatic shoulder."

"But we can't, Mrs Corkish. The road is blocked by felled trees. I tried to get up the glen from our cottage. I couldn't get more'n a hundred yards. It has to be by sea."

May's face was now almost as grey as her coat. Matthew looked at Jem helplessly. What was the matter with the woman? She was island born and bred. Why was she so afeared of the sea?

"We must get back," he pleaded. "Amy needs you. She's on her own. She is desperate. You must come."

May looked towards Jem for support. "Can we not get the men from the village roused? Could a group of them get us through to Port Grenaugh?"

Jem shrugged helplessly. "Maybe? But how much time might that take?"

"I cannot go by sea," May stated firmly. "You return that way, Matthew Kinrade. I will be with you as soon as I can."

Matthew felt like ranting at the woman, but the look in her eyes prevented him. Besides, what was the point in wasting time? "I hope we will see you soon as possible," he said tightly, giving Jem a frantic glare. Fat lot of help he'd been. "I'll be getting back."

Matthew stepped out into the night again, his head pounding with anger. He stamped back down the hill, hardly noticing that the rain had abated, though the wind was still strong and gusty.

By the time he'd reached the jetty his concern was all for Amy. Whether May got to her in time or not he had to get back as fast as possible. He looked up, at a lazy moon struggling through the receding clouds. "You're doing your bit, anyhow," he said, glad of the wan light gleaming on the bouncing water. He leaned down to untie the Nessy and jumped aboard. He began to raise the sail.

124

"Hi, Matt. Wait! We're coming!"

The faint shout was near overwhelmed by the gusting wind. Matthew looked towards the hotel and saw Jem and May stumbling towards him.

Matthew flung a rope hastily ashore and hauled the vessel back to the jetty. He longed to ask how Jem had persuaded May to change her mind but by the look on their faces he thought it best not to ask. Jem hefted May into the boat then leapt in himself, landing with a thump that made the craft wallow alarmingly. May shrieked, but Jem grabbed her round her capacious middle and pulled her towards the centreboard. "We've sent the Gelling boy to rouse Farmer Cannon," Jem said. "He and his men will get through one way or another."

"That's wonderful," Matthew cried, turning the vessel. The Nessy bobbed like a cork as it met the currents at the mouth of the cove. Matthew had no time to observe his passengers; he was too busy, though he could hear May's whimperings of fear.

"Don't worry," he shouted over his shoulder. "Just keep your heads down and hold on. The tide is ebbing. Once we've rounded Santon Head it will be plain sailing!"

"Plain sailing," May Corkish raised her eyes heavenwards. To her gaze the sallow moon had a crafty look. "Oh Jem," she moaned.

Jem, nervous himself, but never in a position to get quite so close to May before, held her in a vice like grip. "You're a brave good woman, May Corkish," he muttered in her cold ear. "Don't be feared. Matthew's a fine sailor like his father."

Imperceptibly Jem felt May relax. Then a greater wave hit the vessel and she hid her head in his shoulder. Jem swallowed nervously, yet there was elation in his heart and as he looked up at the moon he thought it had never looked more benign.

"There," Matthew shouted a few moments later. "We've rounded the Head. The tide's with us. We'll be ashore in less than twenty minutes."

"Thank the Lord," May muttered, and moved imperceptibly away. Jem released his grip just a little. "Twenty minutes, darlin' girl. Why not enjoy the ride?"

May froze.

"Sorry," Jem whispered. "I've been wantin' to call you darlin' for a long time. It just sort of slipped out. You don't mind, do you?"

May shivered, spray was beating over the boat and the wallowing motion was making her horribly queasy. "Maybe not," she muttered. She would give Jem a piece of her mind later, when she was on dry land, if that wonderful state ever came about. She should never have come. It was fearful, thinking about all that deep dark water and the only thing between her and certain death being a few thin planks and a layer of paint.

Imperceptibly she drew closer to Jem, and he, wisely, accommodated her but kept quiet.

Matthew's heart was thudding as they neared Port Grenaugh. Though he'd been away from Amy little over an hour he was now more fearful than ever for her well-being. A welter of pessimistic 'what ifs' mounted in his mind, so that by the time he was tying the vessel at the slip his head was almost bursting with anxiety. "I'll run ahead," he shouted. "I must be seeing if she's all right. You follow…" he hared off before Jem had helped May from the boat and they never heard his throwaway instructions.

"It's grand to see a concerned husband," May said shakily as she straightened herself and tucked some windblown tendrils under her hair net. As she gathered her bag and prepared to follow Matthew she gave Jem a glare. "You should not have forced me to come, Jem Stevens."

Jem's face fell.

"But, lad," May's mouth curved in a tremulous smile. "I'm glad you did." I've been feared of the sea for far too long and I'm too grown a woman for my fears to get in the way of my duties."

Jem beamed. He'd been full of admiration for the strength of character May Corkish had shown during the brief but frightening voyage, being well aware of the reason for her aversion. As a girl she'd seen her father and brother drown in a shipwreck within sight of land, and had not set sail since.

"I'd be a concerned husband, if you'd have me, May darlin'," he said, taking her bag from her and tucking May's hand beneath his arm. "So that's something to think about while you're delivering this babby."

126

"Jem Stevens!" May cried. "Let's keep to the matter in hand and don't dawdle." She shook off his grip and stalked ahead. But she had a smile on her face which remained there until she reached the cottage where Matthew was dancing in the doorway looking frantic.

"Hurry, please, Amy looks exhausted. Please help her."

From that moment May Corkish took control. With a firmness born of years of experience she bade Matthew to 'calm himself' gave Jem a look that said. 'Keep him out of my way' and after having handed Jem her coat she rolled up her sleeves and headed for the bedroom. At the door she turned. "Boil plenty of water and get towels and cloths ready, and Jem; I'd like a cup of tea and a slice of bread and butter to settle my stomach.'

After only a few moments Amy's wails died away though the constant murmur of May's voice continued. Matthew heaved a sigh of relief, and then started as a gurgle of laughter came jointly from the women.

"What's going on?" Matthew said, filling the teapot with a shaking hand. "Is she having this baby or not? She looked so dreadful when I got back I was afeared, Jem. Now they're in there joshing."

"Don't fret, Matt," Jem said, taking the tea and bread and butter to the bedroom door and knocking.

May received it with a nod and turned back to Amy who was wincingly anticipating another bout of pain. Jem hurriedly averted his gaze and closed the door, yawning. He wondered when this strange night might end. He'd been more than ready for bed when he'd spied Matthew's sail. Now here he was miles from home drinking tea with an expectant father while in the next room the woman he'd proposed marriage to was delivering a baby.

Had he really proposed? Or was it just a dream? Jem yawned again. He was too tired for sensible thought.

"Would it be all right if I kipped on your settee? I'm fair worn out."

"Yes. I'd get you a blanket but they're all in..." Matthew gestured just as a shriek of pain came from the bedroom. Matthew's face paled. "I think I'll go outside," he said, slamming his tea cup down and hurrying to the door. "I'll cut some kindling. It'll keep me busy."

Matthew cut enough kindling in the next hour for himself and several neighbours. Every time he stopped he thought he heard Amy cry out again so he picked up another log to split. Eventually he had to sit down, through pure exhaustion, and as he looked wonderingly at the huge mound of chopped sticks, his eyes sticky with weariness, he wondered whether parenthood could ever be worth such anguish and moreover, why did people keep putting themselves through it?

Then Jem appeared with a wide grin on his face. "Come on, lad. May's sent me to fetch you to meet your family."

"What?" Matthew said dazedly. He tried to jump up but found he could hardly move, and he dropped the hatchet, almost on his toe. "Is the baby here?"

"Come and see," Jem grinned broadly, leading him by the hand.

Matthew burst into the bedroom. "Is it here? What is it?"

May beamed at him from the bedside chair, one well wrapped bundle in her arms. Amy smiled weakly from her pillow, another well wrapped bundle tucked close beside her.

"It's not a baby," Amy said softly. "It's two. Two dear little babes, a girl and a boy."

"Oh Amy," Matthew said, "you clever, clever girl."

May gently handed Matthew her bundle then she pushed Jem ahead of her out of the room.

"You did well," Jem said admiringly. "You're a real capable woman, May Corkish."

"I am that," May nodded, accepting this compliment as nothing more than her due. Then her dark eyes lowered demurely for a moment. "But I'd be glad to have a man to depend on again, Jem."

Jem stretched his arms wide.

"There are two conditions," May smiled warningly, as he advanced.

"Anything, anything, my love."

"I'll not live at the hotel with you. You'll have to move into my cottage."

"Agreed. That'll be no problem."

128

"And I'm not going back in that cockleshell boat. So you'd better get out with an axe and cut through all those felled trees, or we'll be here for ever."

"That would suit me," Jem said, pulling her onto the settee.

"Now, now! That's enough! The young couple need some peace. They'll get little enough with two babes to care for. We can't stay here in their way."

Jem glanced at the ticking clock on the mantle. "May dear, it's three in the morning. I'm weary. You're weary. With a bit of luck by morning the farmers will have cut a way here so let's just take a rest and give thanks for what we've got and what we're going to have."

May glanced into Jem's agreeable face. Somehow, without trying, she'd attracted another good man's love. She was a lucky woman. There would be work enough to do in the days to come. There was always a crop of babies to deliver at this time of the year, and the little family in the next room would be needing her frequent help and guidance.

"Yes, you're right," she said, and subsided gratefully into Jem's embrace.

In the bedroom, with his arms round wife and babies Matthew sleepily gave thanks for his children's safe delivery and his own survival. With determination they had all come through a night of great danger. Now with the storm, the tide and the night receding he was aware of new responsibilities settling on his shoulders. Amy was now a mother, he a father. Matthew felt a surge of wonder at this incredible change. The sea might still lure him and, he hoped, would long provide the means for his livelihood, but from now on his family must always come first.

RATTLING TO RAMSEY

Ballaglass

The Corony, Maughold was the location of my first ever published short story. Long before I wrote it, or moved there, I spotted my fictional protagonist, a young entrepreneur of about seven years of age, returning pop bottles for cash in a baker's shop in Peel. At the time I pondered as to why the child needed all the pennies he so eagerly scooped from the counter.

Months later, ambling along a footpath near The Corony I spied a tip of half buried bottles near a ruined cottage. My story took shape and eventually appeared in "The People's Friend," as 'The Treasure.'

The Ballaglass area is a wildly lovely unspoiled district, and the location of my favourite 'visualisation' scene, a place to imagine when in need of inner calm. By merely closing my eyes I can summon up the scent of sun-drenched grass, and hear the drowsy insect hum of high summer against the backdrop of a wildflower scattered hidden pathway.

On stormy nights when gales would rage, battering our home and the encircling trees as though we were on a ship at sea, or as if a wild Buggane was rampaging upon North Barrule, I would snuggle beneath the bedclothes and think of cottagers long ago, and how on such nights they must too have shivered in their beds. Thankfully morning always restored 20th century normality and across the fields the reassuring sight of the daily MER tram, rattling to Ramsey.

Still feeling decidedly shaken, though a long night had passed, I stood by the window and stared out. The words of Walter's letter lay on my mind like a badly digested meal; intractably lodged and impervious to indigestion remedies, though I had taken a substantial dose of milk of magnesia during the early hours.

Frowning, I searched the dear familiar view, my view, as I had long regarded it, for guidance, whether divine or human I cared not, I merely desired to resolve this dilemma which had been laid before me with such unexpected abruptness.

No God given sign swept the serenity of Nature, yet my mental discomfort lifted a fraction as I gazed at the unchanged landscape. Such a view could not but uplift anyone's spirits.

Summer had waned, the leaves on the encroaching garden sycamores were already gilded at their edges and the blowsy blooms in the borders needed dead heading, yet they still looked beautiful, the roses hanging motionless, as if captured by a camera shutter, lurid yellows, beautiful pinks, heart rending reds, their sweet scent still evident though portending their imminent decay.

I felt akin to those roses, whatever bloom I once enjoyed has faded, though this is of scant concern. I have never been precious about my looks, and cannot understand those who are. God bestows upon us what we deserve for the most part and until this unexpected recrudescence into my past I have generally quelled remembrances of my youth, with its ever onerous embarrassments. I have instead enjoyed the vagaries and mild enjoyments of each day and consider myself a contented woman, being blessed with a sturdy constitution and a sensible mind. Also, although my means nowadays are limited I am able to enjoy all that I wish, to maintain my restful, though sadly selfish life. Should this be heinous in the eyes of the Lord I will no doubt find out, in due course.

131

Sighing I glanced once more at the letter, with no wish or desire to re-read it. The bold sentences were etched ineradicably in my mind; the lavish language, the ambiguous entreaties resonating like clanging bells in a long silent bell tower.

I inhaled slowly and calmly, mindful of the ever rushing passage of time. Staring into space, or at the view, no matter how dearly loved, would provide few answers, nor would it get the note which I had been writing to Marie finished, so I settled at my desk and once more took up my pen.

I formed a sentence, misspelt a word, crossed it out, and then, temper risen, for I dislike untidy compositions, gave vent to a loud, 'Damn! Why has this dratted man disturbed my peace after all these years?'

Answer came there none. The house, as always, was silent.

'This will not do,' I cried. I take pride in my letter writing, always with fountain pen and mid blue ink, I take pains to maintain a firm, attractive, legible hand and it irks me to amend an error, as the end result is always unsightly and to my mind shows disrespect to the recipient.

That reaffirmed, I crumpled the sheet of paper, dropped it in the wicker waste bin and laid a fresh sheet of the cream vellum I favour squarely on the blotter. By which time any enthusiasm for this bread and butter missive had utterly evaporated.

I leaned on my elbows, and stared, beyond my rampant garden to the patchwork of fields beyond, to the fields that slope on either side of the central valley, to the white painted cottage almost hidden by a fuchsia hedge in the far distance, beside which the trams run each day to Ramsey; this calm, unchanging landscape which has been the backdrop to my life for sixty years. Could I ever envisage leaving it?

It is so lovely. The developers have not advanced in this direction yet – desecrating the countryside with their mean looking houses and apartments – fortunately the geography of Maughold is unsuited to sustained expansion. I trust that as long as I live it may remain so.

Though my mind still shied from facing 'the letter,' my instinct being to push its intrusive nature away I willed myself to be strong. After all, I had to give Walter an answer. He would expect one, and soon.

I suppose, deep down, I was flattered. Flattery, however, is pleasing only if one seeks it and yearns for change. What need have I for a different way of life? I find new experiences excessively tiring. This is not due to age, as a small child I felt the same.

As dear Papa enjoined, the receipt for a long, happy and productive life was 'Rest and quiet' in abundant doses. Indeed those three words encapsulated Papa's lifelong advice for all ailments or situation of adversity. Father practised as he preached, though he was a busy man he rested often and regularly, as did Mother. Their habit, passed on to me, ensured a perennially peaceful home; the quiet calm of it ever welcoming pre-lunch snoozes, afternoon naps and evening dozes, followed by soothing, restorative night time hours full of tranquil sleep.

An apt name for our solid stone residence, full as it has long been, of soothing somnolence, would have been 'Tranquillity.'
Its actual name, 'Ballaradcliffe' - home to the Radcliffe's - is nevertheless also perfect, as this fine 'thirties construction, of sandstone and granite, solid oak floors and gracious lofty rooms was Father's life long statement of achievement.

'And how proud he was of it!'' Despite my mood a smile relaxed my face as I pictured him, all those years ago while speaking at our select house-warming dinner, when I was but a child. His expression that day was one of near incoherent gladness, he was so pleased and happy, and not a soul gathered resented that gladness or begrudged his achievements.

Father was rarely a self-regarding man, though indisputably smug regarding his business acumen, and why not? Over many years Edwin Northfield Radcliffe earned an Island wide reputation as a clever and successful entrepreneur. His decision, in his maturity, to erect a family home in his favourite Island location was a commendable venture, both for us, and for the local building community. Father's contribution to the design of Ballaradcliffe was imprinted in every brick and upon every roof tile. He was determined that our home and garden should ultimately blend harmoniously into the landscape, and cause no disturbance to this district he loved so dearly and with which he was well acquainted. His humble God fearing parents had reared Papa, along with four siblings, in a tumbledown sod cottage at the side of Ballaglass Glen. Father knew every inch of the countryside about here; he loved this area with a passion. He had been born in abject poverty yet had achieved greatness.

Papa's aim regarding our home was more than achieved, for even now when I say where I live people look perplexed and remark, 'Well, well, I never knew there was a house there.' Maybe, with time and nature's assistance the brash new developments on this blessed isle will also ease themselves into a comfortable permanence - if they don't first fall down.

Abruptly aware of my wool gathering I lifted my pen and swiftly re-wrote my note to Marie. Its purport was the acceptance of an offer of luncheon prior to the annual Ramsey Cottage Hospital garden party later in the week. I was touched by Marie's thoughtfulness. It would be pleasant and convenient to lunch together before our joint attendance at the Garden Party, which is an event that neither of us has missed for near forty years. Nothing, certainly not my unexpected missive would make me miss a social event of such allure.

Once the envelope was addressed and stamped I dealt with other correspondence and pushed Walter determinedly to the back of my mind. Which was where he should reside, I recall thinking, maybe meanly, though almost immediately I recanted. He had taken trouble with his letter. I should reply to it, and fully, in my own good time.

Luncheon suited me on the day of the Garden Party for another reason too. I had an appointment at my bank that morning, and as financial affairs always disturb my equanimity, I should require a brisk walk, such as would be necessary to reach Marie's house, and a quiet meal before the exertions of the afternoon.

I sealed the final envelope and put the letters ready to post later. That done, I veered my mind once more past Walter and permitted myself a further wallow in nostalgia.

When I said Papa 'built' this house the term was of course, a euphemism. What I should have said was that Father had sufficient wherewithal to employ the best builders in the district to follow his instructions and design. I was a but a tot at the time, yet I recall one or

134

two visits, long before the house was complete, when realisation dawned upon me that this wonderful play area of half built walls and exposed joists would one day become my home. I remember the thrill that this thought prompted, and my triumphal march across the bare boards of the ground floor while I chirruped my delighted approval, but then my puzzlement as to how I should climb to my bed in a house that had no staircase.   Ultimately, of course, a staircase was built, and not just any staircase but a very a grand affair, with lavish risers and treads and a curling oak banister planted in the hall like a serpentine tree. The lobby had a scrolled pattern on its lower walls and a dado rail that as I grew became nearer, and then receded as I reached maturity. The floor was finished with blue, white and ochre tiles, these commenced on the floor of an impressive porch - where an aspidistra was soon enthroned in a capacious majolica pot. There were kitchen and scullery areas in the basement, two large reception rooms on the ground floor as well as a conservatory, cloakroom and flower room. Four bedrooms above, a bathroom, three long attic rooms, and a lofty roof space for storage.

It was a house styled to impress, to advertise my father's riches and worldly success; Imposing to look at, impressive to visit, draughty to live in and horrendously expensive to maintain, as I found later, to my cost.

After Mother, and then dear Papa died I often thought to move, the responsibility of maintaining Ballaradcliffe being a constant battle, blocking draughts, redecoration and repairs an expensive drain on my limited resources, plus, as the years progressed having regularly to place buckets in strategic places in the roof space until after one particularly wet winter when so many buckets were in use I felt I could start a hardware store come spring, I finally faced up to my responsibilities and got the roof fixed.

I think it was then I vowed definitely to sell up, yet as always something held me back from taking even the first step of getting a valuation. At heart I had no desire live in any other building, and as this is my bequeathed home, why should I move?

I still feel the same.

Or do I?

Having an inducement handed on a plate, so to speak, a chance to live in a different manner, perhaps to take occasional trips to 'that other isle' has unsettled me. Content as I am in my well known and loved life and location it might be agreeable, before too many more years have passed, to visit other countries, if only to compare them with the undoubted beauty of my dear home island.

Once I would have leapt at such a chance.

I shook my head briskly. No, I would not. I would have given it due consideration, I have never been the type to leap at anything.

Now - do I feel any frisson of excitement at the chance of travel? Actually no, my immediate reaction is a resigned weariness even at the contemplation of packing, let alone the driving, sailing and interminable train journeys involved in getting across England, let alone the continent.

As for air travel, I have not the constitution. I could not have taken the strain, even as a young woman. I have no intention now of being searched or corralling myself into a metal box for any destination, save heaven, and then my box will be good solid wood, preferably mahogany.

Ah, you say, maybe this is old age talking. But what is wrong with being realistic? If one has not developed wisdom in one's old age what has been the point of life? Besides, good common sense tells me that by stepping out of my well-trodden life path I may very well sacrifice all that I hold dear in the way of contentment and end up in a ditch of disillusion. That is too high a price to pay for a fleeting period of happiness with any mortal man.

That decision prompted a further review of my life. I settled more comfortably into my chair. I had no need to rush towards my sandwich lunch. It was but steps away and already prepared.

Nowadays I live entirely on the ground floor. Quite inexpensively some ten years since I had the reception room to the left of the front door divided, and a bathroom put in, not quite so inexpensively, but it was well worth it. My bedroom is the other half of the divided room.

I live, eat and write my correspondence in the remaining right hand spacious reception room. It has the best views across the garden and the valley. An aspidistra still survives in a pot in the lofty porch, which is now my kitchen. With the front door blocked, sink, cooker and cupboards installed by a skilled local builder the finished result is more spacious than many apartment kitchens I have visited and as it was designed with convenience in mind it is always a joy to use. I enter and leave the house through the conservatory. Damp and dank this is nowadays but full of atmosphere; I will not change the conservatory – ever.

It was in the conservatory that I enjoyed – or endured, maybe, the one romantic interlude of my life. It was a very long time ago; I was barely twenty, when a certain young man offered me his hand in marriage. Whether through nerves, or ardour, this youth threw caution to the winds, overstepped all boundaries of politeness after making his request, by virtually throwing himself at me, though gaining nought, for the crash of a pot of lilies he knocked over as he clutched me to him brought Father and Mother to the door and drove the young man to flee in mortal terror. I received no letter of apology, and though I hoped for some years that he might offer again, my hope gradually died, with no great regret on my part.

I was disappointed at the time of course, more for my parents than myself, yet I gained comfort from the fact that from that day I was not entirely naïve in the ways of the flesh. For long after I dwelt upon that hot pink face so close to mine, the feel of his hard body against my bosom and wondered what might have happened had that lily pot not fallen.

Occasionally afterwards when I sat in the clammy dankness of the conservatory, my mind wandered, or rather my imagination did, as to what might have occurred, indeed what should have occurred had I enjoyed a less sheltered upbringing.

Such thoughts have long since waned and they never did depress me, or cause me to mourn my loss, if loss it was. I may well have enjoyed less happiness had anything come of the encounter, than I can now look back upon. Though I have led a somewhat solitary existence it has been delightfully amenable. Quiet days, calm peaceful evenings with the curtains drawn, the lamps lighted and the congenial company of my radio.

By choice I do not have a television. I read, write to friends and intermittently as a hobby, I make notes regarding my funeral. A few times a year I attend a church locally, or in Ramsey, just to keep my face known, rather than with any fervent sense of faith. Time passes serenely. And every Friday, winter or summer, I go by tram, 'rattling to Ramsey.'

Do I really want to tear myself from these well tried and loved routine habits? What fears rush in, even as I contemplate the very possibility.

The expression, 'rattling to Ramsey', originated with Father. Though Papa favoured steam railways rather than electric trams, once he was appointed as a Member of the Manx Electric Railway Board, as a matter of duty, as well as enjoyment, we took family tram trips regularly. In those days the service was more frequent, so that even for business meetings in Douglas Father would travel by tram, and have his car meet him at Derby Castle. 'A waste of money,' Mother would comment sourly, though Father did not resent this. He held his counsel and would in moments sweetly restore Mama to good humour.

There, I am smiling once more. How dear Mama delighted in complaining. It was, I believe, her chief pastime. Not that she was an uncaring mother, far from it, she was capable of great tenderness to me, and any in trouble, yet when humour was being handed out Mama had clearly been looking in a quite different direction. Mother lived an entirely literal life and one had to respond in kind, especially as she grew older, or she took offence. Father knew how to deal with her every nuance, and their affectionate interchanges were always cordial and charming. Often I wished he were not quite so understanding, or forgiving. Mother could be utterly infuriating; many a time I had to hold my temper, though I endeavoured to allow for her sensitivity and usually gave way.

In my younger days I once attempted to analyse my parents' relationship, which seemed curiously inapposite, though there was clearly great affection between them and that I envied. As I matured I occasionally sensed I intruded on their closeness, but I bore this with equanimity. Ballaradcliffe was a happy house, a fine place to live and as I girl I felt carefree. I had my regimes, of reading, regular walks and correspondence. I did a little sewing, though my stitches were invariably clumsy and I assisted Mother in the kitchen when we were between maids. My greatest joy was my regular and always interesting outings to Ramsey Town where I would visit the library, do a little shopping, pay calls on friends and walk in the Mooragh Park.

"Are you rattling to Ramsey, today, Ettie?" Father would regularly ask in the old days at Friday breakfast. "I shall be lunching at the George, would you consider travelling in style with me?"

Father would accompany this question with an indulgent smile. He already knew my answer, but he liked to tease.

I always maintained my dignity. "Yes, Father, I am going to Ramsey by tram as usual. Thank you for your offer, but the tram route is so pretty this time of year."

"You say that whatever the season!"

"Well, it is true," I would smile, rising from my simple repast of tea, fruit and dry toast. I was never a great breakfast eater. Mother was not like me, I can see her now, frowning and fussing with her napkin, remnants of toast, boiled eggs and sticky marmalade on her plate and the tablecloth – she long suffered from 'morning nerves.' 'You will get me a nice book this time, Ettie? I could not take to the last one.'

"I will try, Mother. You should come yourself to choose. Would you like to?" I knew the answer, but I always waited, and hoped.

'No, not today, perhaps next week, I have so much to do.' Again the hands would fiddle, with hair, with cup and saucer, with the rose bud vase which customarily each day held a fresh bloom. She would evade my gaze. Father would look anxious and pat her hand. 'Ettie will choose you a good book this time, dearest. I'm sure.'

'I will,' I would say and hurry off to get ready. No matter how often I went, and still go, to Ramsey, it is always an enjoyable outing. It is such a pretty town and has all that I require in the way of living necessities, as well as beauty in abundance. The Mooragh Park must be one of the most magnificent leisure spaces in the British Isles.

It is quite a walk to the Ballaglass tram stop. Whereas once I would have considered it but a step I notice it nowadays. Of course there is a bus I could catch from the main road to Ramsey, but as I've said before, I prefer 'rattling.' The day I cannot manage the walk to Ballaglass will be a sad one indeed. Then, and only then, I may call a taxi to take me to the tram stop.

What? *Travel* into Ramsey by taxi? Never!

Wearing my stoutest shoes and always carrying my mackintosh, just in case, along with shopping bag and purse I would rush off, full of the energy of youth, equipped too with shopping list, library books and depending on the weather, hat or sunglasses; sometimes both. Nowadays I set out in a more leisurely fashion, but still well accoutred, our Manx weather is notoriously changeable.

Ballaglass Halt is a popular stop off for school parties, prior to tramping through the splendidly scenic glen. Often the tram is crammed with youngsters as it rattles along the line from Dhoon. Yet once the children have alighted I will usually be able to find a suitable outside seat and settle myself for the journey. When it is excessively blustery or wet I will venture into the covered car, but being in the fresh air is still my preferred mode of travel.

In the old days I knew all the regular passengers well, as they me. There were many 'Good morning, Henrietta' greetings from acquaintances as they boarded at Ballajora, Lewaigue or Belle View and if I was lucky someone familiar would engage me for morning coffee, lunch or afternoon tea.

Those were the best days of my life, in my early twenties and thirties, though I did not suspect it at the time. I was full of hope for the future and there was always a spring in my step, for I felt secure in my place in the world. I was Henrietta Radcliffe of Ballaradcliffe, Corony. All the Ramsey shopkeepers knew me and knew that any account I ran up would be promptly settled. I wasn't indulged by my parents but Father liked me to be well turned out and was never more pleased than when I bought a new outfit and showed it him. What a lucky girl I was. What a silly girl, too, when I look back I was so sure then in my naivety, that one day my prince would appear, maybe 'rattling to Ramsey' too. Tall, dark and handsome, a little like father, but maybe more distinguished, a moustache, perhaps, and a knowing gleam in his eye. Oh, how I had pictured him in my girlish dreams. How many times had I searched for him amongst the crowds of holidaymakers at Ramsey Station? I had been so sure, so very sure. Yet I had done little to encourage callers or male friends. I shunned the church socials and rarely visited the picture houses in Ramsey, of which there were two. Now few folk can even recall the Plaza or the Ramsey Cinema.

And now, that my 'prince,' or at least a man purporting to be he, has re-appeared on my horizons, I am at an utter loss; at my time of life do I want – or need - male companionship? It would sorely disrupt my 'rattling' routine, and I do have my friends to consider.

Each week I take coffee or lunch with Lily Taggart or Marie Swales, depending on who can manage one or both. They are each as old as the hills – well, we are all about the same age - I suppose - and over coffee, or lunch, in the Mitre or the Court Café our chat is of acquaintances who have recently died, have become hospitalised, or worse, are in nursing homes. Apart from such 'old lady' catching up exchanges we still have a giggle, at ourselves, and others, especially when our chat reverts to 'the old days,' and we are as up to date as we need to be. We take for granted the fact that Lily is 'on line' and has, according to her, several hundred 'Facebook friends.' M'm...

Marie and I remain true to the printed word and we are avid library users. Such a valuable resource, a library, and Ramsey Town Library is excellent.

Lily and Marie are my oldest friends; we attended a dame school together in Lezayre Road - the building now long demolished of course. I doubt if any of us imagined then that our girlish friendship would bond us for life. Marie is a widow, and becoming frail. Lily is a tough character, a lady farmer owning substantial acres in Lezayre; she lives for her land and animals. Hence she cannot often manage coffee or lunch. Afternoon tea time is just about possible in her busy daily schedule.

Marie is becoming a cause for concern, I believe she is showing signs of dementia, though maybe I am too, and no one has the nerve to say. I've certainly become absent minded lately, though I maintain my routine determinedly and always take sufficient exercise, both for my mind and my increasingly rickety limbs.

Yes, what about my limbs? At my age I'm in no state to go gallivanting across, the whole idea is utterly preposterous. Oh dear, that does make me sound parochial, but then, I suppose I am, I am certainly not used to 'thinking -beyond the frame' - yes, I too, have become aware of the tiresome present day jargon, even on the BBC!

141

Thinking of travel, can I see myself on a cruise ship, conversing with all and sundry? No, no, no. And what if one got ill? Some of these cruise ships have very poor hygiene.

A little cossetting might be pleasant though. My income is not what it was, what with the dire bank losses and interest rates unworthy of mentioning. A little luxury might be nice in my declining years before...

Urgh! My insides crawl at the idea of having to go into care. I have every intention of passing away in my own home, whatever my decision; HE must understand that at the outset. My funeral will be a simple affair, there will be few to mourn and I do not intend to bankrupt myself by providing for a lavish send off. HE can do that, if he chooses.

"No!" I could practically hear Papa's outraged voice.

"Good gracious, Henrietta Radcliffe, where is your self-respect?"

I felt like grovelling. 'Sorry, Papa,' I murmur swiftly. 'I allowed my emotions to get the better of me.' The fact is that after so many years of quiet life I can hardly envisage real excitement.

Humph! As Papa often remarked, 'Does excitement necessarily lead or even contribute to a contented old age?'

More than likely not, if what I've read in the newspapers is to be believed, or even half believed. I was never credulous and any newspaperman's business is to sell his news sheet, often at the sacrifice of truth. I regard newspapers as a soporific form of fiction for those of limited minds.

Ah, a waft of scent has blown in on me. Did I mention the lilacs? Some late blooming flowers are still out, great blowsy blossoms that hang over the driveway and waft their musky perfume through my windows. Also, judging by the noise from the roadway, some quarter mile distant, it is again the time when motor cycles clog the Manx roads and crash into each other with dispiriting regularity. Not the major festival, the period of the Tourist Trophy races, which are held in June, but the Manx Grand Prix, a series of races for those of more amateur status, I believe, though I am not at all versed in the niceties of motor racing.

The racing will not affect my foray into Ramsey, as the tram line does not cross the racing circuit, though extra care may be needed while crossing from the tram station to Parliament Street.

I find my stick an advantage in getting about of late. I am not lame, indeed I feel that for my age I have excellent balance, but my limbs are not so spry and a stick is a simple way of warning that I expect some extra consideration. The stick was Papa's and has a handsome horse head bone handle.

I decide to stir myself and take my walk; otherwise I should miss the post. I will consider some pros and cons in the open air, maybe the delicious late summer scents will imbue my churning mind with more ordered thoughts.

They did not. I spent another restless afternoon and night and was glad upon rising that Friday had arrived. Nothing was decided, save that I felt more troubled than I'd felt for years, which was in itself troubling. I was in two minds whether to confide in Marie. A trouble shared, they say, but Marie is so confused lately that she might not be able to take in my words and then I'd feel cross and that would make me and her tetchy. Oh dear.

The tram ride was as usual, a cheerful experience, the jogging movements and the rattle of the bogey wheels always reminds me of Papa's voice calling, 'cheer up, 'Ettie, cheer up,' as he was won't to chant when as a child I got into what he called, my 'high or low dudgeons.' Dear Papa.

The twin cars were well loaded when I boarded at Ballaglass but I was fortunate in finding a suitable outside seat although it was next to a stalwart leather clad motorcyclist who, save for a nod in my direction, hid himself behind his video camera for the entire journey, I trust he enjoys his film when he gets home, though I feel he might have gained more impression of the beauty of the landscape had he laid his camera down.

As always I noted as many details as possible of the passing scene, I like to keep up to date with what is going on in the district. A surprisingly large extension is being affixed to Mona Ville, which will look entirely out of proportion. The residents are new, I know, from

England. One of the huge Victorian villas at Port e Vullan has been covered in scaffolding, though that will be for repainting, I assume. A new 'For Sale' sign has popped up, between Belle Vue and Ballure, on the tiny chalet bungalow where dear Maggie Thompson lived with her son, maybe they've moved, or did I hear she'd gone into the Grest Home? I must enquire. Best of all, as we rattled through that Escallonia overhung stretch before Ballure I saw that the shabby little house there is as at last in new hands, by the look of the skip and workman's van outside. Most satisfactory, it was formerly such a pretty property.

The sea, glimpsed between the houses, looked calm and glassy, promising good weather, with luck. The pier looks much as ever of course. Another bone of contention, when will its future ever be settled?

I was pleased to arrive, amidst the hustle and bustle; I'm not so old that I don't get pleasure from seeing visitors enjoying our lovely island, and now, a short walk to Parliament Street, where I must attend my appointment at the bank.

Afterwards, standing on the step and surveying the street, my nose twitches with the scents of Ramsey, all so familiar. New cut grass, gardeners are busy tending the Court House lawns. Fishy scents – of nets, catches and rusting tackle from the quay only a street, away, a smell so bracing it lifts my spirits, which had been somewhat lowered by the recent financial interchange.

Still, no point in dwelling on my monetary situation, it could be worse. Now that I have a state pension I am able to keep my head above water despite the sorry tidal loss of investment income. Father would be appalled at the present financial situation, and the casual attitudes prevalent in banking institutions would have shocked and saddened him. I am glad he lived, and died, in a different age.

I shall now stroll to the library and after exchanging my books it will be time to set out for Marie's house. I have already decided to avoid the traffic-noisy route by way of Bowring Road. I shall take a peaceful amble through the Mooragh Park. I deserve a little indulgence. Walter's letter still lies heavily on my mind. Without its weight, now that my bank business is concluded, I should have felt carefree and happy towards the rest of the day.

It is still splendid in the Park, so nicely kept, so spruce, as Father would have said, and the recent ban on dogs was a sensible move. It must have made this lovely green space so much nicer, and safer, for kiddies. Just look at that little tot. What a darling. It must be a joy to have children and grandchildren...

I suppose, had I been robustly adventurous I could have sought a more exciting, fulfilling life. Yet with all the hindsight I can muster, I do not regret a single step of the life I have pursued, and besides, it does no good to repine. Each life presents its own challenges and I suspect I was born to be a spinster. Moreover I believe I have made the very best of being one, though no doubt some think me a weird old stick.

There are five sailing yachts on the lake and a variety of row boats, or are they paddle boats? There is much jollity in them, children laughing, and adults struggling with oars. I recall Father and I having a battle on the Mooragh Lake one hot Sunday afternoon when I was but a girl. He was no rower, nor was I. The boatman had to rescue us eventually, but Father took it all in good spirits. We were sated with sun and laughter by the time we reached home. Fortunately Mother never knew of our adventure, I fear she would have had hysterics had she been with us.

There is such serenity in the view from the top of the path here, where I have often stood to catch my breath, looking across the lake towards the mountain road, the hill of Barrule at the forefront and the reach of hills to Snaefell, Manxland's only mountain, in the distance.

Ramsey's claim to royal fame in the shape of the Albert Tower, named after Queen Victoria's consort, peeping over the tree clad slopes of Lhergy Frissel, always fills my heart with pride in my homeland, as does the dear familiarity of the buildings of the town, the swing bridge and the harbour.

As I look down at the reflection of the neatly trimmed bushes, and the café, reflected in the gleaming water I think about how many

145

times I have stood here, lost in admiration; since I was a but a young child.

Oh dear! Views are all very well, but I do feel hot. Has that path grown steeper? I feel so very thankful that Marie's house is now but a short distance away. Wilting, I plod onwards, the muffled sound of loudspeakers being tested in the Hospital grounds growing louder with each pace. I hope the crowds turn out in force for this afternoon's effort. It is the most important fund raising event of the year for the Cottage Hospital amenities fund.

One thing is for sure, the organisers have deservedly been blessed with a grand day, with ice cream clouds drifting across a sky of deepest blue. Perfect enough so that I may safely leave my mackintosh and umbrella at Marie's this afternoon.

Marie's lunch was delicious. Cold salmon and cucumber salad, raspberries and tinned milk after; I was pleased not to be offered cream, Marie knows it upsets me. She looks well today, and is quite 'with it.' Maybe I was mistaken about her. She seems no more confused than I. Lunch cleared and the dishes washed, we set out.

Well - what a glorious afternoon. By four o'clock we were quite exhausted. I had chatted to countless acquaintances and visited each stall several times. I took part in several tombolas, guessed the weight of a sweet looking baby doll and tried for a win on the bottle stall, but came away from all empty handed. Sensibly I avoided the cream and iced confections on the cake stall, plumping for a fruit filled cut and come again loaf. Marie purchased a dear little china 'Peter Rabbit' from the White Elephant stall, and then promptly dropped him. Luckily he survived his grassy tumble and I daresay he will appear on Marie's mantle next time I call.

Lily showed up about three thirty, bought a sheaf of tombola tickets, shared a table with us and drank innumerable cups of strong tea and demolished several strawberry scones lathered in butter. It is always heartening to be with Lily, she reminds me that once we were once spritely girls and in our hearts still are. She very kindly offered to drive me home, I, in return, hoping she might have a sensible viewpoint on 'the letter' promised her supper but she refused as she

146

said she had to get the 'beasts' in and 'do' them. I didn't delve into the details of what she might be intending, sometimes Lily reveals details of her daily routine that one might prefer not to hear.

I was immensely grateful for the offer of a lift though and actually relieved she did not want supper. If she had accepted, what would I have given her? An omelette? Probably, Lily would have turned her nose up at my planned sardines on toast. In all events I could look forward to our journey back. I liked catching up with Lily. She lives at such a pace, with her many agricultural interests. I don't know how she keeps so tirelessly active and I have great admiration for her.

Marie won nothing in the tombola, nor did I. Lily won two bottles of 'plonk' – her description and a set of dainty dinner mats which she pressed into my shopping bag with instructions to 'get rid Ettie, what would I do with such frightful things?'

I happily pushed the mats into my capacious shopping bag, I judged them rather charming and if I didn't use them I would donate them to one of the charity shops in Parliament Street at a later date.

There was a terrific crush at the end of the afternoon, crowds of folk all struggling to get off the Hospital grounds at once. Marie held back. 'Go ahead,' she waved us away with a tired smile, 'I can take my time, I've only got to cross the road.' We left her willingly, and it was only later that I remembered my mackintosh and umbrella. Luckily I always have spares at home.

Lily propelled me from behind, using me somewhat like a battering ram, until we breeched the crush. She was as always, determined. 'Brace, up, Ettie," she adjured, 'that's it, keep shoving the blighters. The car's over there. Hey, just look who's behind that huge woman, isn't that Walter Grenfell?'

'What!' I turned quite weak. Nemesis was almost upon me and I was far from ready. I squinted in the direction she had pointed, and I could indeed see a huge woman, I could not see Walter.

'There, in that old Rover, look!'

I peered distractedly as a stylish, though rather shabby vehicle fired its engine. I'm quite well versed on car marques, especially older ones, it comes from Father's interest, I suppose. I peered and peered, but could not make out the driver as the sun was glaring on the windscreen.

'It can't be,' I murmured hopefully, 'you are most likely mistaken.' But as the Rover accelerated and passed us Walter's maudlin, current-brown eyes looked straight into mine and I felt a tremulous shiver run through me.

'Told you,' Lily grinned as she held open the door of her battered 4 x 4 – 'and he saw you. Oh, watch that bag on the floor, 'Ettie, it's got a dead pheasant in. It's a bit high but it will do the dogs for tea.'

'Ergh! Lily, it reeks. What are you doing carrying a thing like that around, and in this weather? Shouldn't it be hanging or something?'

'Mebbe,' Lily crashed the car into gear and drove off at a lick, narrowly missing the wing mirror off a red VW Golf timidly pulling out. 'Told you, it was Walter Grenfell; I'd heard he'd moved back. Cripes, what a turn up for the books. Look out, Ettie, he might come calling again.'

'Don't be utterly ridiculous, Lily,' I prevaricated, too mortified to admit to his communication. 'His pash for me was forty years ago. He's probably long forgotten he ever knew me.'

'He hasn't. He asked after you not long ago.'

'What? When? You never said.'

Lily gave me one of her beaming smiles, and I noticed how good her teeth were still. I attributed their healthiness to all the red meat she voraciously devours.

'He was married to a girl I knew in Cumbria. They bred Labradors. I got a dog off them, once. She died, I think. The girl, I mean, not the dog, though that went for the chop too eventually.' She ground through the gears once more. 'Didn't like to say I'd met him. Didn't want to stir up the old, you know.'

'Oh Lily, I'd have liked to know.' My insides felt strangely constricted, though it was probably just that last slice of Battenberg I had eaten. 'You should have told me.'

Lily revved the engine fiercely; we were through Ramsey by this time and climbing the steep rise of Slieau Lewaigue. 'Least said,' she shrugged, hurling us around a bend. 'He was a snake. Shouldn't have let you down like that.'

I giggled. 'He was shy. So was I. Such a long time ago now, no point dwelling on it, is there?' I settled back in my seat. I wouldn't confide in Lily. I would write to Walter that night and say 'forget me, I've already forgotten you,' even if I hadn't.

'I've had a lovely peaceful life. A husband would get, would have got in my way.'

Lily winked. 'They're good for some things.'

'Oh Lily, don't. There's no point, is there. Besides, I would have hated to share a bed, with any man.'

Lily swung the car into the narrow turning to Maughold. 'Yes, they hog the duvet, no matter what. That's why I plumped for celibacy, ultimately.' She sneaked a sideways look at me. 'Two husbands under my belt. I should know.'

'You should, you wicked girl.'

We drew up, laughing. Our laughter died as we slowed and turned into the lane. Parked alongside my overgrown gateway was a shabby green Rover. It was empty.

'Oh Lily,' I gasped.

'Oh crikey,' Lily giggled. 'Shall I come in with you?'

'Em, no, but, wait for a moment or two, if you don't mind.'

' 'Course.'

I pulled my shopping bag, heavy with library books and cake from behind my seat without disturbing the bloody pheasant, which had attracted several buzzing flies, straightened up and pushed open the gate. It squeaked loudly, and I was glad I'd not oiled it recently. He would know I was coming. Whatever Walter had to say he would, hopefully, have ready. I trusted I could deal with him politely, though I might need to summon all my resources so to do.

As briskly as I was able I marched up the sparse gravel of the weed choked path.

For years I had not given Walter a thought, and never imagined we would meet again. Nor had I wanted to, though it would be interesting to see how he had aged, and he would no doubt be curious about me. I hoped he had not been watching me covertly as I

149

tripped about at the garden party. Mother would have deemed that behaviour unworthy of a gentleman, and I concurred.

'Henrietta.'

He was standing on the steps to the former front door, which of course I did not use, the porch now being my kitchen. What I saw as I peered, without the benefit of my specs, was a middling looking, middling sized, unremarkable man with untidy grey hair. His grey check sports coat and light trousers, pink shirt and a deeper pink tie were slightly more remarkable. Pink! The Walter I recall would never have worn a pink shirt.

'I trust you don't mind my impromptu visit,' he said, sounding rather fussy and old womanish. 'I knew you'd have got my letter by now. I was passing, en route to Laxey where er – I'm staying. Maybe for good, not sure - well that's why I've come, of course.'

My heart thumped, but not unduly uncomfortably. Nowadays I doubt if Walter could set anyone's heart thudding. I stayed at the foot of the steps, smiled and held out my hand. 'It's good of you to call, Walter.'

He had to descend. Slowly I noticed, and with a slight limp.

'Is it?' His warm fingers touched mine briefly, then we both looked away, but as his wrist dropped his other wrist jerked and that gesture suddenly conjured him again as the young, rather weakly handsome man I had once – what? Desired was too strong a word.

'So many times I intended … I really should have let you know… erm. Oh dear, what can I say? I know it's almost a lifetime late, but may I apologise?'

His voice, so long unheard, suddenly conjured up a long ago church social, and Walter hanging on my every word. I recall being mortifyingly unsettled by his attentions. It had been like conversing with a new species. I had blushed and stammered, I remembered.

Goodness, just a word or two had stirred such long ago reminiscences. His eyes too, though they were far from the young eyes I remembered. They looked old and tired, like mine.

I came to with a sigh. I was weary, my head ached and truly I would have preferred Walter to recede once more into my memories. But, sheer habit, an instilled code of ingrained politeness and courtesy urged my fingers into my handbag for my keys.

'You must have a cup of tea, Walter. We could have it in the …' how nearly I said the conservatory, 'in the garden, or maybe in the house as the sun is lowering.'

'That would be nice.'

'Come this way.' I led him to the conservatory door. He spoke not a word as he followed me through the plant heavy gloom; though the lingering memories of our encounter must have beset him as they certainly beset me.

So hard on my heels was he that on entering the kitchen he practically fell on me. As my tired feet, in my best summer shoes, were already throbbing I panicked that he was going to step on my corns. Involuntarily I thrust out my hands, dropping my handbag, to shoo him back. What was he up to, coming so close? 'Invading my space' I believe it is called nowadays. It was utterly beyond the pale, however it might be labelled.

'No, Walter, this is my kitchen. Please, wait in the hall.'

An astonishing thought swept into my tired mind. What if he'd come here to finish off what he started all those years ago? I couldn't bear that. Nor would I permit it. If need be I should take my cast iron frying pan to his head.

One glance at his shiny visage, however, relieved me. Walter looked no more fit to ravage a fit spinster than a wet flounder. I reduced my forbidding flapping to a twittery flutter, and forced a smile.

'Let me show you my sitting room while I make tea, Walter. You'll be comfortable there.' I led the way across the hall.

'Oh, I see, this is very different,' he said, in a somewhat patronising voice as I ushered him through.

I surveyed the calm sunny room, with its pleasing pastel curtains and bright pictures. Of course it's different, you silly man, it's more than forty years since you were here, I glowered inside, while outwardly I maintained my mother's favoured social lift of countenance as I gestured to the Examiner and a comfortable seat. As a girl Mother had drilled me in all social niceties of expression until they became second nature. Poor Mother, she would have been shocked at the dearth of polite society I had enjoyed in my later years, though as it has been by choice she might have accepted the matter with

151

resignation. Even in my youth there were 'characters' who though, like me, did not match certain standards, were still accepted by those who mattered. Nowadays everyone and no one seem to matter.

'I shall not be many minutes,' I informed Walter, pleased that I had left the room tidy and with the cushions well plumped.

I hurried to the kitchen, filled the kettle, reached for a tray, and then started violently as Lily's face appeared at the window.

'Are you OK?' She mouthed through the glass. 'Do you need support?'

I pushed the frame open. 'No dear, I'm fine, thank you,' I whispered. 'I'll phone you later, let you know how I get on. Off you go, get your beasts settled.'

'Good luck,' Lily winked wickedly and marched off. I smiled after her and reached into a cupboard.

'Was that Lily Swales? She brought you home, did she?'

'What? Yes!' I swung round crossly. 'Walter, I almost dropped these china cups, and they are Mother's best. Please, wait in the other room. I've had a busy afternoon and I'm a little tired. I'll be through in a moment.'

My asperity had the necessary effect. Walter beetled off. I sighed, hastily laying the tray and cutting three not very even slices from the new cake I'd bought, though two were for show. I had consumed sufficient cake and scones to last me a week.

Once the tea was brewed I carried the tray into the sitting room with a feeling of near serenity. I felt myself ready to set Walter swiftly on the right track and see the back of him.

He had, ostensibly at least, been reading the Examiner, but threw it down as I appeared. I tried not to exclaim, seeing as the paper was considerably rumpled by his action. 'How long are you staying on the island, Walter?' I felt quite like my Mother as I spoke. She was always especially agreeable to those whom she disliked, or even despised.

'Erm – oh, milk and sugar please, three spoonsful.' Walter responded, as I poured. 'Oh, I'm not sure, how long, that is. My - friend and I are staying in a holiday cottage at Laxey, practically on the beach.'

'How delightful, have you come for the fishing?'

152

'Sorry? Thank you.' He accepted his cup. I held out the cake plate. 'Oh, yes, rather.' As I expected he lifted the larger piece and took an immediate bite. 'M'm, good cake, no er, no. We don't like fishing.' He shifted in his seat and I noticed that his small paunch overlapped his trousers in an ugly manner. I immediately imagined Papa's disapproval.

'Look, 'Ettie, let's get down to basics. You read my letter?'

I nodded, colouring slightly, despite my determined coolness.

'Has it done the job? Cleared the air, so to speak?'

I felt confused. 'I am sorry? Was that your intention?'

'Yes, 'course. Why, what did you? Oh dear, I said some of it was over the top but er...' He looked down and gobbled the last few cake crumbs as though he was starving. 'M'm, well,' he spluttered vaguely.

'I thought on the whole it was well composed,' I said coolly.

'Did you? I'll tell Sheila, she, er...' He gulped, his goldfish eyes widening unedifyingly.

'Sheila?'

He gawped, like a mouse caught in a trap.

'Whom, may I ask, is Sheila?'

Walter pulled out a handkerchief, well laundered, I was pleased to note, and mopped his glistening brow, though the beads of perspiration did not appreciably lessen.

He shrugged. 'It was her idea, actually, I'd told her – you know – and she said, even though it was years ago that – what happened, happened, well, she said it would be best to clear the air with you. After all, we'll be bound to run into each other, won't we?'

'Will we? Please elucidate, Walter.' Shakily I lifted my cup to my lips. 'What status has this 'Sheila.'?'

'She's my – partner, is Sheila.'

My hackles rose. 'I beg your pardon?'

'Sheila Tiplady.' Walter gave his forehead a last dab, pocketed his handkerchief and reached unprompted for a second piece of cake. 'My present paramour, so to speak,' he laughed uneasily and took a large bite. 'I told her all about you,' he said, spitting crumbs between words.

'You're not married to - Sheila?'

153

'We've decided not to bother. After two trips up the aisle we're both a bit wary.' His currant eyes darted past me as if seeking an escape route. 'My second wife cleared off last year. My first died, a bit of a tragedy that,' he looked towards me munching hopefully, as though I might ask for an explanation.

That, however, was the last thing on my mind. My insides felt as though they were turning to lard. An unlikely analogy but that is the only way I can describe the sensation of feeling weighed down; even my tea cup seemed heavy. With the utmost care I laid it on the lace edged tea cloth in the tray. 'But your letter? You were so... excessively erm; I hate to use the term, ardent, but that it how I, mistakenly I see now, construed it.'

Walter, gaped, then giggled, 'You didn't? I thought she'd laid it on a bit thick, but Shiela said I should be fulsome, even after all these years.' Walter wiped his fingers on his trousers, even though there was a perfectly good paper napkin by his plate, and then he grinned at me, as though he was enjoying a really good joke, at my expense.

I sat, appalled, my back ramrod straight. Mother would have been greatly impressed by my erect deportment. She would not, however, have been impressed by my situation.

'I say, could I have that last bit of cake? I got to the 'do' a bit late and the old biddies wouldn't hand over anything for free.' Walter was already reaching his fat fingers but I leapt to my feet and snatched the plate out of reach.

'I beg your pardon? You refused to pay for your refreshments?'

'No, well, yes. I'd already forked out three pounds at the gate. I was glad Sheila hadn't come too. She decided to get her hair done. I just dropped in with the hope of seeing some old cronies.'

'I see.' I laid the cake plate on the sideboard and walked to the window. Thank God the view was still upliftingly serene. I swung on my heel, having quite forgotten about my sore feet. 'The event was to raise funds for the cottage hospital. Do you not give to charity?'

'I always say charity begins at home, don't you?'

I moved closer, my heart pounding. 'No, Walter, I do not. But then I have already decided that we have nothing in common anymore.' I was barking by now. I could hear myself, just like Papa used to bark when he was very cross.

'I admit to being startled to receive your letter, especially as I construed that for some strange reason, after this unconscionably long time you were repeating your advances to me. It is now apparent that I was seriously mistaken.'

'What?' Walter was dabbing at an errant sultana on his plate and gave a sputtering guffaw. 'Christ, no! As I said, I just wanted to clear the air. We're planning to settle in Laxey, and as we're bound to meet, well - you know.'

I didn't, so I said nothing.

'Yeah,' he continued, while my temper rose. 'Sheila's Dad was a tram driver in Salford when she was a kid. Laxey takes her right back. She's always loved trams and she's taken to Laxey like a duck to water. Couldn't be better, could it?'

My heart was thumping, but now with blessed relief. Thank the Lord; Walter had not been trying to foist himself on me. He had merely been trying to smooth his social path. He has assumed, mistakenly of course, that I still have enough 'clout' in society over here to make things awkward for him and his inamorato.

I smiled benevolently upon him.

'Finally I understand your motives, Walter. How sweet that you are coming to live here again, though you need feel no anxieties regarding myself. Until I received your letter I can honestly say I've not given you a thought in several decades. If you hadn't written I would probably not have known you, had we passed in the street.'

He smiled uncertainly. 'That's er - handsome of you, 'Ettie,' he smiled, though his brow was creased. 'Sheila encouraged me to write, formal, like. Clear it with the old ducks,'' she said, in the generous way she has, but that's Shiela all over. You'll like her, you will, Ettie. She's the salt of the earth. Give you the coat of her back, she would.' He rubbed the side of his nose meaningfully, 'and, lucky for me, she's loaded.'

I stood above him. He started to rise.

'No!' I exclaimed, breathily, sounding again just like my mother. 'Don't stir yourself, Walter. Let me clear away.'

He sat back, smirking.

155

I smiled graciously as I picked up the still well filled china tea pot. I knew the settee covers were washable and that the tea was by now quite cool. Nevertheless, as I emptied the pot over his head Walter Grenfell squealed and yelped like the little rat he had always been.

'Now get out of my home and don't darken my doors again,' I cried, as he scrambled to his feet to escape. Still holding the teapot I chased him through the hall and the conservatory. As he limped, dripping, up the path I shouted a final warning.

'Don't you dare board the tram on Fridays. That is when I go to Ramsey. Or I'll throw something even more horrid over you and your Sheila.'

Trembling, yet extraordinarily elated, I stripped the settee, put the covers in the washing machine and tidied away all traces of Walter's visit.

After that I lifted from my kitchen cabinet a tin of sardines in olive oil for my supper. 'How nice,' I thought, as I tugged the ring pull open and revealed the neatly laid fish inside. 'I may now continue with my delightfully selfish, orderly life.' On a whim I walked to the drinks cabinet and poured a small celebratory sherry. I sipped it while staring peaceably from the window.

I resolved that after my simple supper I should ring Marie and Lily. I might, or I might not tell all about Walter, but what I most certainly would do, would be to arrange a rendezvous for Friday next, when, as ever I would be 'Rattling to Ramsey."

THE END